ETM:
His Life

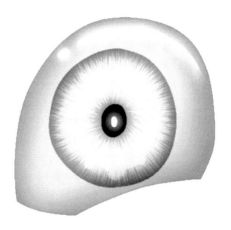

A J Webster

Acknowledgements:

My Brother, Midnight, for the artwork.

Newman Additional Resource Staff for help and support.

My Dear Friend, Anastasia, who encouraged me to carry
on writing when I was about to give up.

First published in the United Kingdom by
Arc Publishing and Print 2021

ISBN: 978-1-906722-83-8

Chapter 1: "The Same Routine"

The darkness of sleep, it was so comforting. That's how he always felt. There was nothing more serene and quiet than the emptiness that could only be felt when he closed his eyes and his mind became clear, everything was just so peaceful in those few hours that he got to experience it. Though, everything has to end eventually and peace is not dissimilar in that regard. Eventually, the warm embrace of sunlight shone through his window and onto his eyelids which immediately pulled him away from his tranquillity and into the real world where such things rarely exist. He just stayed there on his bed that he swore had shrunk from last night as he silently cursed the morning for taking his unlimited supply of freedom. As he laid in bed for another few minutes, he pondered what to do... after all, it was only a matter of time before they appeared once again. Almost as if it was on cue with a schedule that was never created, they crept their words into his head once again.

"So, are you just going to lay there forever and do nothing or do you actually want to be productive today?" They asked which caused him to roll his eyes. Was he really going to have to endure another full day where they just will not leave him alone? All he wanted at that moment was peace and quiet... that's all he ever wanted ever since they started speaking to him but he never got it and at that moment, he doubted that he ever would find it again. He sat up from his bed as he had now completely given up on trying to reclaim his lost tranquility and he decided that for once, they may be right. As he stared around his room and tried to collect his thoughts which did not exist, he looked up at them. Their face was exactly as he remembered it, though he could not describe how it appeared... at least, that's what he told himself. The truth was that he could at least attempt to describe them in great detail

3

but it would never be enough to make himself or anyone else understand what exactly he was seeing... but then again, maybe that was wrong. Maybe the truth was actually that he could describe this being perfectly and everybody would immediately know what he was talking about if he told them about it but he was too afraid to mention it to anyone because he knew that nobody would listen or even acknowledge him.

In all honesty, he could not remember what was the truth anymore. He had told himself so many lies about what he was dealing with on a daily basis to the point where he couldn't differentiate truth from fiction any longer. "I thought you said that you were going to stop thinking about me." They stated with their cold voice as he couldn't help but imagine a smug grin being plastered over their face as they spoke those words. Slowly, he lifted his legs out of the sheets and onto the floor as he used what felt like was all of his energy to simply stand up and look out of the window and onto the cold, emotionless world that was disguised by layers of bright colours and warmth. "You shouldn't go out there, don't you remember what happened last time? I remember it clearly; they were all staring at you as if you had done something wrong but you only ever just passed them on the street. If you go out into that world, there's only pain waiting for you." They insisted constantly as he began to change into his usual clothes. Their words were reaching his ears, in fact, they were damaging his mentality to the point where he could physically feel it, he just actively chose to ignore it.

He took step after step until he reached his door which he pulled open without a second thought despite his emotions telling him that he should just fall asleep once more. Every movement that he took simply came down to muscle memory as he had gone through these same circumstances day after day for a few years now, how could he not just memorize every action that he has to make to last through the day? Were there people in that house that worried about him or might've wanted to stop him from proceeding to where he was going? There may have been more people there that witnessed or heard him leaving but he didn't care at that point, he wasn't even able to tell if they were real or if they were just an illusion or hallucination that had been created by his mind so he could attempt to convince himself that this world was better than he originally thought. One step after another, he made his way down the stairs and towards the front door and all he could think about was whether or not they were still following him. "Oh, don't worry I'll follow you wherever you go. I'm not going to let you go out into a dangerous world like that all by yourself." They explained as he could practically hear the smile forming across their face as the insincerity in their voice was painfully obvious.

He held out his hand before he carelessly placed it against the cold and firm door handle before he pushed it down and stepped outside as he closed it behind him and continued out onto the street. The entire world seemed empty at that moment, not a soul in sight which only made him all the more comfortable. "Are you sure that you're the only one around? There could be somebody right behind you." They conveyed in a voice that sounded as genuinely worried as they could possibly manage even though they were obviously faking it. That street was basically his entire life, the houses looked as dull and bare as one could possibly get and the people only made it worse as most of the adults tried their best to ignore him whilst the children just silently judged him for no reason. His mind was only focused on his destination as he passed countless of identical buildings that lined the streets as the warm sunlight wrapped itself around his body to try and distract him from the inevitable rush of negativity that was swiftly arriving... in fact, he could feel it starting at that very moment.

"I'm telling you, it's a bad idea! If you go there again then it'll only be worse than the last time and it'll carry on getting worse until you break!" They began yelling so that he would pay attention. He heard them... and that's when the stress began once again as his head began throbbing with wave after wave of pain. Despite the agonising pain that this stress headache was causing, he did his best to ignore it as he knew that it would only show how weak he was if anybody witnessed his suffering. Once he looked up, he noticed how he was at the park that he had been heading towards for a few minutes... or was it a few hours? Possibly a day? The time didn't matter to him, the months passed like days and the days passed like seconds in the last few years of his life so it didn't really matter in the slightest. This park was full of tall green grass that had not been disturbed for months along with a path that circled all the way around it that was mostly covered by the aforementioned greenery although he had come here so often to the point where he had memorised every single crack in the stone so he didn't have any problems in navigating through it.

At last, he reached the centre of the park that was surrounded by a small, black metal fence that contained two swings, a bench and a small climbing set with a slide at the end that was obviously intended for younger children. "Well, you're here, now what are you going to do? Don't tell me that you came here just for a lazy excuse to not get anything done." They asked with a condescending tone. He simply ignored them once again as he sat down on one of the swings that he was obviously much too big for. They surprisingly fell silent after this action as he began thinking about everything that had happened for him to get to this point. All of their past trauma, the lack of people who actually cared. Everybody always said that school was unbearable but he didn't see anybody in his school that everyone ignored and denied success as much as they did to him. Not only that, there was also the fact that he was constantly running off just like he did not even a few minutes ago and the fact that nobody even seems to care about what's happening to his mental state... and... and... a tear fell from his face.

"Everyday, it's just the same routine. You get up, you think about what you're doing before you do something as an excuse so you don't put in the effort to get your life together and finally, you promise yourself that you'll get everything sorted on the next day. That's what everybody else thinks that you do... but I understand." They explained in such a way to the point where he couldn't even tell if they were trying to give him advice or make him feel worse. He once again elected to ignore them as they were clearly wrong about him. It wasn't his fault that all of this was happening, he can't control his emotions, he couldn't have made any of this better no matter how hard he tried. His thoughts quickly began to race through his mind as he could no longer describe how he was feeling with one single emotion nor multiple emotions at once, it was as if he was feeling everything and nothing at once as a growing emptiness clawed its way through his very being. One thing snapped him out of his constant downwards spiral of feelings... and that was the simple sound of the chains on the swing next to him rattling as somebody else sat down beside him. They simply gasped as they attempted to make some kind of pessimistic remark but all they could do was watch and listen as the two of them sat side by side seemingly unaware of the presence of the other.

He managed to lift his head to see who it was that had disturbed the only peaceful place that was left for him in the hellish world... only to find a girl about his age with short brown hair who was wearing the average clothing that all of those who silently judged him did. A shirt, trousers, jacket and shoes all in black or a dark grey colour. How did she know about that place? Why had she come here at this exact moment in time? "I've told you before; this world and everybody in it hates you. She most likely saw you here and decided that you'd be most uncomfortable if she were to stay here." They attempted to convince him. He was inclined to believe everything that they had just told him... but there was something that was causing him to have some doubts about what he had just heard. Perhaps this one person was different?

"Well, if you're so dead set on attempting to communicate with this girl then you'd better at least say something before this all gets way more awkward than it needs to be." They expressed which confused him even more as to which side they were taking... was talking to this girl a negative or a positive thing? He attempted to open his mouth but he couldn't even manage to do that simple task... it was as if his past trauma rushed in to prevent him from speaking. This only got him thinking about the situation more, why would his previous experiences with conversations be getting in the way of this one? Is it because talking to this one person would erase all fear and doubts in the future that involved this kind of stuff? There was only one way to find out, if he could just push past this one obstacle in his mind then maybe, just maybe, he could finally be rid of everything that holds him back.

He looked over to the girl who was staring in the opposite direction, he very slowly opened his mouth before he started forming the words within his mind before finally, he attempted to speak. "Stop it! I can't do this anymore! This isn't a good idea, just get out of here before she notices you!" They suddenly shouted at the top of their lungs which stopped him right in his tracks. The words disappeared within his head as he could no longer even make a sound. It was as if that everything on that day that had led up to that moment was just randomly erased from reality without warning. Everything went silent... except for their incoherent babbling as their words became nothing but a set of awkwardly and seemingly nonsensical string of thoughts. "Why would they do that? It's my fault isn't it? I don't want to die!

Why does everybody ignore me?" They spoke like a maniac as he was attempting to comprehend every piece of information that reached his ears but it was clearly an impossible task.

That chaotic and endless nothingness continued to ravage his mind as they continued to ramble on for what seemed like an eternity before the silence of mind and the insane gibberish were erased by a few simple words. "Hey, are you okay?" The girl simply asked which practically froze time for him as it had been so long since he had heard a single word that was directed at him that didn't come from... them. He was completely speechless as he simply lifted his head up to see the girl before he glanced into her deep blue eyes before quickly looking away. "You're not much of a talker, are you?" She inquired which left him in complete shock once more. Why was a girl like her willing to spend such a long time speaking to somebody who barely even existed in the minds of anybody anymore? All he could do to respond was to shake his head to which the girl nodded in response. "I understand that, I have those moments in life when I just want to be silent. I don't mind. My name's Emily." The girl explained in a sympathetic tone which made him feel slightly better even though he knew that she didn't completely understand.

"You don't mind but I do, we were fine until you arrived you moron!" They yelled despite the fact that Emily wasn't able to hear them. "You know, it feels quite unnatural to see somebody like you. You're feeling so many negative emotions to the point where they're practically emanating from you." Emily explained as she seemed quite curious about him for no discernible reason. Was that the reason that so many people hated him? Did nobody else feel that amount of negative emotion other than himself? He always thought that everybody normally felt how he did but considering what Emily had just said, he wasn't so sure anymore.

"You're not helping!" They shouted in another pointless attempt to let their voice be heard. Emily looked at him as he had not looked away from the ground for quite some time like he was lost in deep thought. Despite what it seemed, he was not thinking about a thing, he was still trying to process every word that had been spoken so far. With a look of slight confusion on her face, Emily looked away from him as she seemed to think for a moment before she turned back and started up a completely different conversation. "You're probably wondering how I know about this place, aren't you?" Emily questioned him to which he simply nodded in response. "Well, I'll try my best to explain. I've always had this weird ability where I can sense the negativity of everybody around me and I try to use this trait of mine to find people like you and help them in whatever way that I can." Emily explained which seemed completely absurd to him. Was he seriously supposed to believe that this random girl had powers that nobody else had? It was clear to him that Emily was just living out a fantasy story that she had made up on that very spot.

"You want to help in anyway that you can? Then leave us alone!" They demanded once again to somebody who could not hear them. Emily's expression seemed to change pretty noticeably for a split second... he could've sworn that he saw a look of shock over her face. What was she shocked about? Was there some kind of monster that was standing behind him that has the innate ability to wipe the memories of whoever had seen it? Did she just remember something that she wants to keep hidden? He looked over to them and they had that same shocked expression, only it was directed at Emily and not him. "I understand if you don't want to talk but I can't help if I don't know anything about you. Is it possible for you to at least tell me your name? I'll focus on what's troubling you later but I at least want to know your name today." Emily insisted as she had a more serious tone in her voice. "Would you just slow down already? You're just pushing your luck further past the line that you've already crossed!" They yelled as they seemed to feel the same way about this that he did.

"I'm being serious, I'm not leaving this spot until I at least learn your name." Emily stated as her face showed just how determined she was. He had to do it, this was his chance, he couldn't mess it up this time or he would forever live in a world with nobody who he could call his friends or his family. As he began to open his mouth once more, Emily's eyes widened as she waited for the answer to emerge. "Just stop! You're name is the only thing that you have left! If you give it away then you won't be yourself anymore!" They shouted which caused his thoughts to stutter for a bit before he persevered through the claims that they were presenting and continued to attempt to speak. "M-My name... is-" He began to say before he stopped... but he didn't stop because of anything that anybody had said, no, the reason he stopped was because he couldn't find an answer to Emily's question within his mind. What had happened to his memories at that moment? There was a vague idea as to what had happened within his head and it was a simple explanation; he had forgotten.

He knew that there was a name that was used to address him at some point but no matter how hard he tried, he couldn't remember it. The fact that he wasn't able to find his own name within the far reaches of his mind was most likely due to the fact that it had been roughly seven years since that word had been used in his presence. Emily stared at him with a face that told him that she wanted an answer more than anything else at that moment but she was searching for an answer that he could not provide. They had gone silent as they seemed to be in as much shock at this lack of information as he was. His mouth moved slightly as his mind struggled to find anything to say even if it wasn't exactly the truth. After a brief moment of silence, he closed his mouth and stood up without thinking as he walked towards the exit of the park.

"Hey, where are you going?" Emily asked which caused him to stop just at the end of the fencing. He turned around to look at Emily, he looked her up and down before he noticed that they had disappeared. His hand twitched slightly when he noticed that they were gone before he opened his mouth and without thinking, he spoke. "I don't know where I can go anymore but anywhere else is better than staying here with you." He spoke in a cold tone and with a dead, expressionless face. Emily looked back at him before she simply nodded as he turned around once more and walked back home to a place where nobody cared about him. What happened to him on that day? It's rather simple; he met somebody who actually cared about him before he messed it all up again, he let it happen again and now he's back to the same routine again. "I'm a failure." He tells himself from day to day... and nobody is ever there to disagree with him.

Those words echoed through his head, a memory of a long forgotten time. "Don't worry, nobody else cares about you... but I do. I will keep you safe, forever."

Chapter 2: "Denial"

Peaceful slumbering, why couldn't it last forever? He only messed up everything he ever did in life and it apparently made everybody else feel negative towards him so he probably would've been better off just staying in the everlasting darkness of sleep. Although, that would be too kind of a fate for all of the things that he has done, his dearly beloved dreaming wouldn't be punishment enough to make him atone for his sins. That's probably the reason why this world carries on pulling him back; he has to atone in whatever way that he can before he is granted the eternal peace that he wishes for day after day. Just like the countless times previous to that moment, his eyes were forced open against his will as the daylight poured through the window and clawed at his skin. False sunlight like that was everything that he deserved, everybody else always mentioned how they were excited to stand in the warmth of the day... then why was it that the heavenly lights that shone down from above felt like they were slowly freezing him to death?

"Why did you do that?" He asked them through his mind. "You're always accussing me whenever something goes wrong in your life, I didn't do anything and you know that better than anybody else." They responded with an annoyed tone. "Stop trying to deny it! You disappeared just before it happened, I know it was you!" He insisted as he got out of bed and stared at their face that appeared exactly as it did yesterday and the day before that. They looked back at him without saying a word before sighing and glancing away. "Well, are you ready to see if today is going to be any different or if it's going to be another repeat that started all those years ago?" They inquired as they stayed in the shadows whilst observing the outside world. "It doesn't matter if I'm ready for it or not, you know as much as I do that this world doesn't care for me. Whatever sadistic gods rule over this world will just make everything worse for me at every possible turn." He replied with the most honest answer that he could think of.

The same routine repeated once again; he got up, he got dressed and he headed outside to a world that hated him. Part of him was hoping that somebody would interact with him on his way to the park because of how Emily spoke to him the day prior. There was no such luck, everybody that he passed by on the streets didn't even look in his direction... not a single one. "It wasn't you, don't worry." They suddenly spoke which confused him. "What did you say?" He asked in his mind as he turned to face them. "I was talking about your sudden aggressiveness yesterday, it wasn't your fault. Don't get me wrong, it wasn't my fault either, I just don't want you to worry about it. Neither of us are to blame for what happened." They explained which seemed to ease his stress slightly. "Thank you." He simply responded with a smile before he turned once more and continued walking.

"Maybe, even if nobody else talks to me or even takes notice of me, then I think I'll be able to stay sane as long as I can speak to you at least." He admitted as he passed buildings that constantly seemed to repeat. "You really think so? Do you really think that you'd be able to deal with me being by your side for the rest of your life?" They asked with a surprised voice. "I'd definitely be able to be with you for the rest of my life." He clarified as he seemed to warp to the entrance to the park in the time that they had been talking. They then mumbled something that he definitely wasn't supposed to hear. "Let's hope I last that long." They spoke under their breath but he still managed to hear them saying it. "What was that?" He questioned them as he turned around and stared straight into their face. They stayed silent as they were shocked that his hearing was good enough to hear them.

"You wouldn't understand even if I told you." They stated as they avoided his gaze. "I don't care if I can't understand, just tell me." He demanded in an annoyed tone as they constantly said stuff like that and he was frankly tired of it by this point. "Well, I mean what you heard me say; I hope that I'll be able to last long enough to see the end of your life. I could fade at any moment and there are certain things that you can do to speed up that process." They explained in a quiet voice. "I thought so... but what are these things that I can do to speed up your disappearance?" He asked without thinking about his words before he had already said them. "What the hell do you mean by that? I thought we were actually finally getting along and then you went ahead and said that!" They yelled after a moment of silence. "N-No, I didn't-" He began trying to explain himself before he blinked and when he opened his eyes again, they were gone.

"W-What in the world are you?" He asked the empty space that they once occupied only to have no answer just like he expected. With nothing else to do but question the existance of this nameless creature that can read his thoughts, he walked along the path that was covered by shrubs and grass as he made his way to that same place once more. As he lifted his head up when his destination became ever closer, he expected to find nobody there and to be by himself once more... but he was shocked to find Emily sitting there as if she was waiting for him. "Hello again." Emily spoke with a weak voice that startled him slightly. "H-Hi, are you alright? You sound a bit under the weather." He admitted as he was a lot less nervous now that they weren't around. "Well, I'm really serious about my promises and I did promise that I wouldn't leave this spot until I heard your name." Emily reminded them. "So, you mean to tell me that you haven't left that seat since yesterday?" He inquired as he couldn't tell if Emily was being serious or not.

Emily nodded her head in response which only made him feel worse about himself. She had sat there for at least twenty hours just because he was unable to tell her his name... how selfish of him. "I'm sorry I made you wait that long, I-I didn't think that you were being serious." He apologised as his voice gradually got quieter. "It's okay, I normally bring food with me anyways because I'm normally outside all day." Emily explained as she gave a sincere smile. "Doesn't your family worry about you?" He continued with his questions which Emily didn't seem to mind. "I'm usually out for two days a week because I like helping the community." Emily replied without missing a beat. "Wow, I bet that if you're helping out that much, people really like you. If only I was ever given a chance to do that type of stuff too." He said with a sigh as his gaze shifted to the ground in front of him.

"Well, I see that you have a lot of emotions that are weighing down on your mind. I can help you through this if you just tell me what's happening." Emily explained as she seemed dedicated to her attempts to help him. "That's the thing; I don't know what's happening. One day I'm just minding my own business and having fun, the next day, everybody is just ignoring me and it doesn't feel like they're intentionally doing it either. Whenever I see them looking in my direction, it's like their mind doesn't even acknowledge the fact that I'm there." He conveyed as he struggled to hold back his tears. Emily just looked at him with interest and confusion, it's the type of stare that somebody would give to somebody when they realise what is happening to them but they have no idea why it's happening. "I'm fairly certain that I can help with that." Emily stated after a few moments of silence.

He just stared at Emily in disbelief as he was fairly certain that she had just said that in order to get his hopes up. "Are you serious? You honestly believe that you're able to make people acknowledge me?" He asked as he was surprised that Emily didn't see how absurd that her claim was. "Well, it's worth a shot." Emily replied in such a casual manner that made him unsure of her idea. After a brief moment of thinking the offer over, he spoke up once again. "I guess we could try it. There will be no harm if it doesn't work. Fine, let's do it!" He exclaimed as he suddenly became really enthusiastic before he began to leave the park. "Hey, wait for me!" Emily yelled which caused him to stop and turn around only to realise that she was still sat on the swing. He stared at her for a moment before he remembered what Emily had told him.

"Oh, right, you won't leave until you hear my name." He stated out loud to which she nodded in response. Once again, he searched the endless pits of his mind for a name that was used to address him in the past only for him to draw a blank. There was only one thing that he could do; tell the truth no matter how unbelievable it sounds. "I... I don't remember my name." He explained as he closed his eyes in the hopes that Emily would believe him. "Okay then, well can you just give me a fake name? It can be as random or as strange as you want." Emily replied with a tone in her voice that implied that she found this piece of information to be slightly concerning. His eyes were kept shut tight as he attempted to think of a new name, one that could be used for him. That name could be anything that he wanted it to be... almost immediately, he had an answer.

"Laroxiam, that's my new name." He spoke out loud which seemed to lift a heavy weight off of his chest. "Well then, Laroxiam, shall we get going?" Emily asked as she was suddenly right in front of him which scared him quite a bit. After recomposing himself and pondering how it is that Emily got so close to him without making a noise, Laroxiam finally gained the courage to speak once again. "Yeah, I've been ready this whole time. Thank you for the heart attack by the way." Laroxiam agreed as he attempted to silence the clear panic in his voice. "Sorry about that, it happens all the time. Follow me." Emily replied as she strolled past Laroxiam and began leading the way towards their destination. "Of all the names that you could've picked, now you have to live with 'Laroxiam'." Their voice suddenly reemerged behind him. Almost as soon as he heard their voice again, Laroxiam began to apologise. "Hey, you misunderstood what I said before, I wasn't trying to get rid of you. I was trying to learn what I could do to get rid of you just so I would know what I shouldn't do!" Laroxiam told them through his mind.

"I know, I was just trying to find some excuse to disappear so that you could be alone with her." They responded with a completely understanding voice... although he couldn't actually tell how sincere their sincerity was. "Speaking of your disappearance, we're going to need to have a chat when we're alone again." Laroxiam stated as he passed more identical buildings that lined the streets whilst at Emily's side. "I didn't do it, I swear." They replied quickly the second that Laroxiam had finished speaking. "You... didn't do what?" He asked as he didn't understand what they were talking about. "I'm not important right now, just pay attention to her, alright?" They practically begged as he could hear their voice becoming shaky. "Are you sure that you're-" Laroxiam began to ask before Emily started speaking once again.

"So, I've only just realised that I never explained where we were going. I'm taking you to an old friend of mine who promised to help me from time to time." Emily explained as a few vehicles began speeding past them on the road. "I bet you have a lot of friends like that." Laroxiam stated as he finally started to feel calm enough to the point where he could act like his normal self around her. "Don't worry, I'll make it so he's able to see you before you leave." Emily spoke which shocked Laroxiam once again as he realised how determined she was. "What's their name?" Laroxiam asked as Emily stopped in front of a small shop on the corner of the street. She simply walked inside of the shop before calling out to the man behind the counter. "Oliver, how have you been?" Emily questioned the man as he looked up from a book that he was reading. "Oh, hi Emily, business is slow as usual but I've got way more than enough to keep me going so don't worry." Oliver responded as he stood up and shook her hand.

Laroxiam took a few steps into the shop to see that it was mostly empty besides a few items hanging here or there. Oliver didn't seem to notice Laroxiam at all which didn't surprise him in the slightest as Oliver was just as faceless and dull as everybody else that existed in that world. "What brings you here today? Are you here to use up one of the many favours that I owe you?" Oliver asked in a joking manner. "Actually, for once, I am here for exactly that." Emily replied as her smile seemed as boring and copied as the hundreds of others that wore it before her. "Oh, I honestly thought that you were never going to use any of the favours that I kept reserved for you. What is it that you'll be wanting?" Oliver inquired almost immediately after Emily had finished speaking. "I just wanted you to meet my friend, his name is Laroxiam." Emily explained. "Laroxiam? Now that's a unique name if I've ever heard one. I wouldn't mind meeting somebody new, where are they?" Oliver wondered out loud as he observed the room.

"You don't see him, do you?" Emily asked with a hint of disappointment in her voice. Oliver gave Emily a strange look and paused for a moment before answering. "Is he in this room? Are you playing a trick where he's hiding in this room in plain sight?" Oliver asked as he wasn't sure if Emily was playing a trick on him. It definitely seemed like Oliver was being genuine when he was implying that he couldn't see Laroxiam. "I mean... you could say that he's hiding in plain sight." Emily said as she was hoping that Oliver would eventually notice. "Well, I can't blame you for trying." Laroxiam spoke bluntly as he sighed before he turned to leave. Suddenly, Emily quickly grabbed hold of his hand to prevent him from leaving. "Let me try one more thing." Emily insisted as she stared into his eyes. Laroxiam didn't have any reason to not allow Emily another attempt so he just simply nodded before facing Oliver's direction again.

"Are you sure that you're alright?" Oliver asked as he seemed concerned for Emily. "I'm sorry, it's just that, for some reason, nobody seems to be able to see Laroxiam. He claims that all of this started when he began to think negatively of the world around him." Emily tried her best to explain. "Oh, come on! Who would believe something like that?" They yelled and Laroxiam had to agree with them, who would believe such an insane statement? "Wait, what did you just say? Negative, what does that mean?" Oliver questioned Emily as he seemed to not be familiar with that concept. "Wow, he must be really dumb if he doesn't understand what negativity is." They stated as they put a hand up to their face. All of a sudden, Oliver seemed to jump backwards in shock as he looked over in Laroxiam's direction.

"Who is that?" Oliver asked as he backed himself up against the wall. Emily looked back at Laroxiam to see that there was nobody else standing behind him. Laroxiam's eyes opened wide with shock as he stared back at Oliver. "You can see me?" Laroxiam questioned him in total disbelief as the features of the faceless person in front of him became clear. Oliver had blue eyes and long, frizzy brown hair. "W-What kind of sick, ungodly creature are you?" Oliver practically demanded an answer from Laroxiam as he seemed to be in a state of panic. Laroxiam and Emily could only look at each other with their mouths agape at what Oliver had just said before being shouted at once again. "Get out, both of you!" Oliver suddenly yelled which caused Emily to obey his orders instantaneously as she grabbed Laroxiam and dragged him outside as well.

Shortly after, Oliver slammed the door behind the two of them before he hung up a sign that read "We are closed." "Well... that was certainly something." Emily stated as Laroxiam could practically see the gears turning in her head as she tried to make sense of everything that just happened. "You don't say." They spoke completely nonchalantly. "W-What even-" Laroxiam was about to ask before he heard loud weeping coming from within the shop. All Emily and Laroxiam could do at that moment was to stare at the shop in silence, fear and confusion as they attempted to comprehend anything that they just heard. During this silence, all that could be heard was Oliver's crying before a woman walked up to the store before she saw the sign and walked away as if nothing was wrong... could she not hear or see anything that was happening?

"I... I think we should leave, I'll talk about it with him tomorrow." Emily suggested. "Yeah, I think that'd be for the best." Laroxiam responded as he began to walk back home with Emily following shortly behind him. He tried his best to erase the memories of what had just happened from his mind but it seemed to be a futile effort as the imagery only became more vivid the more he thought about it. Then, he began to jump to many different conclusions at once... he always did that in situations like this. Maybe the reason that Oliver reacted the way he did was because Laroxiam's existence was just that horrifying to everybody who doesn't see him? Perhaps enlightening Oliver to Laroxiam's presence also made him aware of other beings that nobody else could see? How could Oliver have not known what negativity was? This entire train of thought was quickly halted by a few simple words.

"I didn't do it, I swear." They stated which caused Laroxiam to pause and turn to face them. "I didn't think that you were the one who did it. You should know that, right?" Laroxiam asked as he stared at the two bright yellow dots on their face which he thought were their eyes. "Are they at it again?" Emily inquired as she faced Laroxiam. For a moment, Laroxiam stared back at her in confusion before looking around only for him to realise that Emily was talking about Them. "Wait a minute, how do you know about them?" Laroxiam questioned her before she simply smiled and beckoned him to follow her as she began walking away once again. "Are you trying to tell me that you weren't aware that she could hear me yesterday? You're so oblivious to everything around you." They sighed as Laroxiam attempted to catch up with Emily.

"So, let me get this straight, you can see and hear them, right?" Laroxiam asked as he ran up to Emily's side. "No, I can't see them. I did hear them yesterday and I heard what they said to you just now though." Emily explained without turning away from the street in front of her. "When you heard them yesterday, that's when you had that shocked look on your face isn't it? That was when they insulted you, wasn't it?" Laroxiam continued with his questions. "That is correct, it did take me by surprise to suddenly hear a voice from a third party when nobody else was in sight." Emily confirmed Laroxiam's suspicions although it confused him as to why she was speaking like that all of a sudden. "Do you know anything about them?" Laroxiam inquired as he was desperate to learn more about this entity that he had been speaking with for a few long years. "Well, why don't you try asking them?" Emily suggested whilst shrugging her shoulders.

Laroxiam thought about Emily's suggestion for quite a while as he never thought of actually asking them himself. He attempted to ask Emily another question... but as soon as he blinked, she disappeared. In a state of utter confusion, Laroxiam frantically observed the entirety of the surrounding area as he searched for Emily but to no avail. "What the hell is happening?" Laroxiam asked himself as he began to hyperventilate. "So, Emily can hear me, she can see you and she can also disappear much like myself. This is very interesting indeed." They spoke as they thought to themselves. He could no longer keep up with the sights and sounds around him, it all started to fade away slowly as he fell to the ground. "Oh, how disappointing." They stated as they stood over Laroxiam's body as everything turned black.

"I didn't do anything! Why are you accusing me? Nothing even happened! How can you even be sure that he saw either one of us?" They asked as the both of them looked back on that moment with concern.

Chapter 3: "Questions"

"Dude, come on, get up already!" They demanded as Laroxiam slowly began to regain consciousness. All Laroxiam could do was groan as he opened his eyes and felt the concrete against his face. "What even happened to you? Did you pass out or something?" They asked as he lifted himself up from the ground. "I don't even know what happened... would you care remind me?" Laroxiam requested as the sunlight shone brightly into his eyes which quickly adjusted to the brightness. "Well, I doubt you would forget the whole thing that happened with Oliver. After that little incident, you went to ask Emily a question and then she just disappeared. The next thing I knew was that your thoughts were scattered all over the place and then you fell to the floor." They explained which caused Laroxiam's eyes to open wide. "Oh, right, I was going to ask if there were more beings like you that only specific people can see." Laroxiam remembered before shaking his head and thinking about what matters more.

"How does she do that? I mean, normal people can't just disappear like that." Laroxiam stated as he rested against a nearby wall until he felt like he should move again. "Well, how do you explain the fact that I can do that?" They asked as Laroxiam held his head. "That's easy, you're just a figment of my imagination, right? You're something that my mind just made up so I don't fall into an endless pit of insanity, that's how you're able to read my mind." Laroxiam explained as he gazed in their direction. They remained silent as they stared back at him as if what he had just said made them completely speechless. Soon after, they began laughing... although they weren't doing it because they had found something funny, Laroxiam could tell that much. The laughing was most likely due to the fact that they were trying to hide how they truly felt.

"Really, that's what you think? After everything we've been through together and all of the emotions that I showed you, you have the audacity to say that I'm not real?" They asked in a deeper voice as their laughs became much quieter. "Well, you seem to always be feeling exactly the same way that I am in my head so I figured that-" Laroxiam began to explain himself before being cut off. "What the hell do you think I am? You think that you and I are somehow the same person in some way, don't you? Whilst that may be true, don't think for a second that I will stoop down to your level even for a second!" They yelled without even trying to hide their emotions. "How could you say such a thing? What have I done that is so bad for you to want to say these things to me?" Laroxiam inquired as he couldn't understand what he had done to be given this much aggression from them.

"You know what you did! Every single time something bad happens, you blame it on me and act like you're some perfect, innocent little angel. I don't even know who you're trying to fool anymore because I'm certainly not falling for it!" They exclaimed which only amplified the stress that Laroxiam was already feeling at that point. "You're not real, if I just ignore you then you'll go away." Laroxiam stated mostly to try to convince himself that the stress that they were causing would end soon. "So, you're running away from the problem at hand again? No wonder nobody pays attention to you, you just make their lives worse." They said out loud which made Laroxiam stop and turn around. "I don't know what I've done to deserve this from you... but whatever it is, I'm sorry. Can we stop fighting now?" Laroxiam requested as he looked them in the eye which made them unable to reply immediately. They seemed like they wanted to say something in those few moments of silence but instead they broke eye contact with Laroxiam as they clenched their fist.

Laroxiam continued to watch them before he had to blink and afterwards, they had disappeared just like Emily and left him all alone. Frankly, all he wanted at that point was to be by himself so he was slightly thankful to find himself in that position. He began to walk down the street once again as his mind strangely could not seem to find a single thing to think about, Laroxiam found this to be incredibly strange as normally, at times like this, a random memory would pop into his head that would be about something he did when he was younger and when people still acknowledged him... although that memory would likely be something that he just wished that he could forget. As he continued to wander, Laroxiam found that his gaze was shifting around much more than usual as he observed his surroundings which had not changed from the hundreds of other times that he had walked that same path.

Laroxiam paused his adventure down familiar roads as he saw that the door to one of the many identical buildings beside him had been left open and that there was somebody working beneath a car nearby. That was the moment when an idea came into his mind. "If people ignore me without even realising it and they can't see me without hearing about something very specific... and they can't hear me in the first place, then can I just do this?" Laroxiam asked himself as he walked towards the open door and peered inside to find a woman with the same basic face as everybody else along with what he presumed to be her children on the floor playing with some toys. He approached the woman who was staring at a television screen that was showing one of the many channels that was just relaying the same information over and over again. With a strange curiosity gnawing at his mind, Laroxiam waved his hand in front of the screen to see if the woman would notice him... she didn't.

After a few more moments of thinking, Laroxiam made his way into the kitchen which was covered in the same white paint as the one in his house. There was nothing of importance that he could see so instead he moved back towards the front door of the building before he spotted something that he could use as a test. On the wall next to the door, there was a sword in a sheath that was hung up... it seemed quite expensive. The children in the other room were also periodically looking over at the sword as if it had some sort of meaning to them. This was the perfect item that Laroxiam could use for this test of his. Without another thought, Laroxiam took the sword off of the wall as it was surprisingly light, he then held the sword out of view from the children. One of them looked over at the wall again to see that there was no longer a weapon on the wall. There was no reaction in their face, no shock, no wonder, no curiosity, nothing.

They didn't seem concerned in the slightest that the sword that was on the wall that they looked at with such intrigue had suddenly disappeared. Laroxiam's eyes widened at the realisation; he could take anything he wanted from anybody and they would not care in the slightest because they ignore him and everything that has had physical contact with him in some way. With a smile on his face, Laroxiam left the building and continued down the street as he attempted to stall for time for the next day to arrive. "Was all of that really necessary? I mean, you just stole from a family!" They exclaimed as they suddenly reappeared once again. "Look, I know it's wrong but I was just doing it to test my theory. Also, they don't care about it anymore so leaving it there would've just made it go to waste." Laroxiam replied as he looked down at the blade that he was carrying.

"I guess that's true, just promise me that you won't steal from anybody again." They requested as they seemed concerned for some reason. Laroxiam looked back at them before nodding and asking a question. "Is everything alright? Was that outburst just like a one-time thing?" Laroxiam inquired as he was hoping for an answer that he wasn't expecting. "I hope that it was just something that happens once, I didn't even know why I said what I did. It just felt like I was going to lose something at that instant. I'm sorry." They responded as they looked at the ground in shame. "Don't worry, I get it; sometimes your emotions just build up to the point where you can't hold them back anymore." Laroxiam spoke with a smile. They just remained silent for a few moments before they spoke up again. "I'm going to be honest; she scares me." They stated as they seemed to look around to make sure nobody was listening... not that anybody could listen.

"Wait, you mean Emily, right?" Laroxiam asked only for them to nod in response. "I personally don't see how she's scary in anyway. Can you tell me what about her specifically scares you?" Laroxiam requested as he seemed to be genuinely interested in how anybody could be terrified of Emily. "Can't you tell? She's trying to get rid of me." They explained with a weak voice. "Emily is trying to get rid of you? You made it seem like it's obvious that she's actively out to get you but I haven't seen anything that points towards that conclusion, maybe you're just being paranoid?" Laroxiam suggested as an idea which seemed to confuse them somewhat.

"No, I'm definitely not being paranoid. The way she looks at me is just so... unnatural. It's like she knows what she wants from me and she knows that there's nothing I can do to stop her from harming you or me." They spoke without a hint of doubt in their voice. "Emily never intentionally looks at you, she can't see you, she said so herself." Laroxiam replied as he clearly didn't believe them. "What makes you think that she's telling the truth all of the time? Why do you take every word that comes out of her mouth as some kind of sign from god?" They asked with a noticeable annoyed tone in the way they spoke. Laroxiam put a hand to his face as he knew that stress was about to start clawing at his life again. As they were about to say something else, they saw how Laroxiam was feeling and decided against it. "I'm sorry." They said once again before falling silent.

Laroxiam began to think about everything that had happened recently and how his life had changed. He did have to wonder; was this change in his life better or worse than everything that was happening before? Sure, he hated everybody ignoring him but was a life where one person knew about him really worth it for all of the confusion that he was experiencing along with it? Then, he thought about Oliver once again which only added to the uncertainty that was growing within his mind. What if, one day, Laroxiam woke up and everybody could see him again? Would they react in the same way that Oliver did? "We should never have left our solitude. Sleep was the perfect barrier that protected us from this world and we abandoned it. Why didn't you listen to me?" They inquired as their fingers curled into a fist and their rage flared up in their eyes.

"What's wrong with you? I've only taken what life gives to me and now you're speaking to me like it's my fault that I'm having a dilemma about whether this is a good thing or not." Laroxiam stated as he shook his head. "Fine, if you want me to be honest, then I will. The truth is, I'm sick of having to sit here and just watch you screw up everything you do! Just when I think that you're about to change, you blame your problems on something else whether that be life, me or anything else in the world and then you carry on telling me that you can't do anything to make this situation any better!" They yelled as their anger seemed to have boiled over to the point where even they couldn't hold it back. "If you really feel that way, do you mind telling me what I could've done to make this life a lot more bearable?" Laroxiam requested as he was clearly tired of this conversation. "Well, you could've just... you... I mean it's easy, you should've just... I'm sorry." They attempted to reply before they realised that there was nothing that they could suggest.

Laroxiam sighed as he thought that they would respond exactly like that but he didn't want to seem smug about it and offend them even more. "Can I just ask you something? It isn't related to what we were just discussing." Laroxiam asked as he stopped in his tracks to turn and face them. They didn't seem like they wanted to talk so they just nodded in response. "Do you have a name? I just find it weird that we've known each other for years and I don't even know your name." Laroxiam stated as they looked at him with a look of confusion. "You're joking, right?" They inquired as they couldn't seem to tell if Laroxiam was actually serious about what he was saying.

"Why would I be joking about something like this?" Laroxiam rhetorically asked. "So you seriously expect me to believe that you picked a random name that popped into your head when Emily asked you about it and you just so happened to pick the name that I use without knowing it?" They questioned as they were clearly showing how absurd the situation was. "You're kidding me, right? Laroxiam is your name?" Laroxiam inquired as he completely disregarded whatever he was thinking about before.

"Why are you surprised? Everything about me is constantly being stolen by others so it was only a matter of time before you took something as well." They stated as their demeanour became quite dejected. "How can you have things stolen from you by others if I'm the only one that even knew that you existed?" Laroxiam asked, completely unaware of the sudden change in their emotions. "I just feel like everybody is going to steal everything about me that matters and then I'll just be another blank slate with no meaning. What happens after all of that? Do I just cease to exist in the minds of everyone just like you?" They questioned themselves only to find that there was no answer. "Are you sure that you're okay? You sound pretty out of it."

Laroxiam spoke as his concern began to rise once again.

"Since when did I tell you that I was alright? How could you have assumed that I was fine to begin with after everything that I just said?" They asked in an irritated tone. "I'm sorry, I just find it difficult to tell what you're feeling. You know that emotions were never my strong suit." Laroxiam replied with a higher-pitched, defensive voice. "I know that you're not good at telling how other people are feeling because you can't read their emotions well but that's no excuse for you being unable to tell how I'm feeling!" They began yelling once again. Laroxiam sighed before responding to them. "I don't even know what the hell you are!" Laroxiam retorted which seemed to stun them into silence. They just stared at Laroxiam in complete silence as if he had commited some sort of heinous crime right in front of them. Laroxiam closed his eyes and took a few deep breaths before looking back up at their face. "Before we say anything more, I need to know one thing; what are you?" Laroxiam asked as he stared into their faint yellow eyes. That complete sense of being lost that Laroxiam could see in their eyes was one that he had witnessed many times before when he woke up and looked at himself in the mirror. He remembered it clearly; it must have been about four months after the beginning of Laroxiam's erasure from everyone's minds, he gazed at his reflection with tears in his eyes only to see a strange black figure appearing behind him... they must have seen the same fear and confusion on his face that he now sees in theirs. They pondered to themselves for what felt like a few minutes before opening their mouth once again. "I don't know, I only know the answers to the questions that you do." They finally replied before disappearing again once Laroxiam blinked.

"There's only so many mysteries that one mind can attempt to comprehend at the same time and I feel like I'm reaching my limit." Laroxiam stated out loud as he knew that nobody would hear him anyways. He was simply left with his own thoughts as he had to wonder; why was everything only now becoming so eventful? It felt like everything had been planned ever since Laroxiam's descent into nonexistence such as Emily being the only one that is able to see him. "Whatever sick and twisted being that is playing this game better be ready when I eventually figure out a way to get to them. This was funny in the first few hours that this whole thing began but now it's just depressing how you're trying to get so much enjoyment out of a worthless person like myself!" Laroxiam yelled out into the world in the hopes that anything that could hear him would react and prove him right... yet nothing happened.

"Curse you." Laroxiam mumbled to himself as he continued down the path only to suddenly walk face first into a brick wall. It took a moment for Laroxiam to process what had just happened as he held his head. He raised his head to look at the obstacle before him and then looked back down, he did this several times until he just came to the conclusion that he must not have seen the wall when he yelled into the empty streets a few moments earlier. Laroxiam shook his head in disappointment in himself before he observed the surroundings to get his bearings on where he was but the fact that every single building was indistinguishable from one another wasn't helping him in the slightest. With a sigh, Laroxiam walked towards the nearest house to check if he could find out where he was from there, if he couldn't... well the people where he lived are virtually identical to everybody else that he sees so it didn't really matter to him if he stayed in a different area for the night.

"Wait, it's night already? I swear it was broad daylight just a minute ago." Laroxiam thought to himself as he stared into the glowing dots in the sky which he never learned the name of... or if he ever did, it was so long ago to the point where he forgot. He looked down at the sword that he was carrying before he decided to inspect it further, he took the blade out of the sheath only to realise that it was made out of plastic. "Of course they would hang a fake weapon on the wall, oh well, it's not like I was planning on using it anyways." Laroxiam spoke to himself as he strolled into the house only to find the exact same interior as the other buildings that he's visited. After everything that had happened on that day, Laroxiam was ready to close his eyes and relive his moment of peace all over again and so he laid on the sofa that was positioned in front of a television screen as he attempted to fall asleep.

Despite every single one of Laroxiam's senses telling him to return to his slumber full of tranquillity, he found himself unable to close his eyes for long without feeling a sense of uncertainty. It was like something nearby was keeping him awake until he had done what he was supposed to do... but he did find himself wondering what he was meant to do in that moment. After a few unsuccessful attempts at sleeping, Laroxiam decided that he'd play along in whatever game that this thing that was keeping him full of stress had in mind. Laroxiam held his head as he sat up and observed the room to see if anything seemed out of the ordinary. The one thing that caught his attention the most was a book that was sitting by itself on a wooden table as a thin sliver of moonlight shone down upon it.

Laroxiam rolled his eyes at how the book was obviously placed there for him to read and he was already annoyed at how his moments of sleep were being stolen away so he quickly got up and walked over to the book before he began to read. The book didn't seem to have a cover like many of the others that Laroxiam had seen, it was just blue, no writing or anything else... just the colour blue. He shook his head and opened the book to quickly skim through its contents and get back to the one thing that he desired the most. "What are you reading there?" They asked which made Laroxiam look up and see that they had suddenly appeared where he was previously trying to sleep. "I don't know, it doesn't have a title on the cover. For some reason, I can't sleep so I just thought that I'd read through this and maybe I'll just drift off part of the way through it." Laroxiam replied as he rubbed his eyes.

"Do you mind reading it out loud? I'm pretty bored as well and it's not like anybody else is going to hear you." They politely asked as they stretched their arms towards the ceiling. "Fine, if I must." Laroxiam replied with a sigh before he turned to the first page. All that was on the thin page in front of him was a drawing of a girl with long and flowing hair who seemed to be in some sort of forest that was covered in snow. In the girl's hand, there seemed to be a long sword with an interesting design; the hilt had a few spikes on it that seemed to make the weapon completely impractical, the blade itself seemed to have pointed edges along the side that made it almost resemble a saw. Unfortunately, the picture was in black and white so their were only a few details that he could accurately make out. Just from the look of the weapon alone, Laroxiam could tell that the story in the book was completely fictional as there was no way that a blade like that was actually used in combat at any point.

Laroxiam turned to the next page where he actually found the title of the story that was written at the top of the second page. "The Legacy Of The Chosen One. What a completely original title." Laroxiam said sarcastically which made them laugh quite a bit. He smiled at them before he looked back down at the book and attempted to immerse himself in the story in the hopes that it would make him fall asleep quicker.

"Now I realise, that story that I read back then was fake after all! It all makes so much sense now!" Laroxiam told himself as he looked back on his past before laughing until he felt like he couldn't breathe anymore.

Chapter 4: "Anger"

The never-ending darkness that he was staring into, it was so peaceful before that moment that he was living through. For some reason, a sense of unease began racing through his mind as if he wasn't alone in the endless abyss. What even happened last night? He couldn't remember. Suddenly, there was a bright orange glow that appeared in the distance of whatever realm that he had found himself in. "No, I'm not ready to leave yet." Laroxiam stated as he turned away from the light only to find that it followed wherever his gaze travelled. Something about this strange light was different than the unpleasant feeling sunlight that chaotically traversed the world outside. This new light seemed to have a rhythm that seemed similar to how his own head was feeling at the time and its light felt exactly how every other person described the feeling of the sun against their skin.

"This feeling, it's so calming. It's like somebody finally understands me... who are you, friend?" Laroxiam asked as he reached out towards the light that seemed to be similar to that of a sunset. The light drew closer to Laroxiam as he embraced the fact that he would willingly reject his eternal peace just to feel the warmth. As he drew closer, Laroxiam could see something reaching out of the light, it looked almost like a hand that was offering itself to him. With a smile, Laroxiam grasped onto the hand before everything quickly became brighter, almost blindingly so. "Hey, are you alright?" A feminine voice asked as he felt his eyes opening. "Get away from her!" Laroxiam heard them yell as he looked up to see Emily standing before him.

Laroxiam looked down at his hand to realise that the hand that he had grabbed was actually Emily's. He jumped backwards with a slight yell only to fall off of the swing and onto the concrete beneath it. "Wait, I'm at the park? What the hell is happening?" Laroxiam asked himself as he held the back of his head. "Oh my goodness, are you alright?" Emily exclaimed as she knelt down to help Laroxiam back onto his feet. "Don't scare me like that, seriously." Laroxiam spoke as he looked around whilst being lifted up by Emily. "I'm sorry, you just reached out your hand and I thought that you were awake." Emily apologised as she smiled slightly. "How did I get here?" Laroxiam inquired after the pain had faded slightly. "Don't ask me, I just saw you here and thought that I should come by and say hello." Emily replied. "You walked here all by yourself, you didn't respond to me or anything." They responded which confused Laroxiam.

"I moved all by myself and didn't answer you, was I sleepwalking or something?" Laroxiam asked. "You only know as much as I do, I haven't seen anybody sleepwalk before so I wouldn't know if that's what it was." They replied whilst shrugging their shoulders. "Oh, right, about that guy that only you can see, did you ask him about what we talked about?" Emily questioned him as she seemed to be more interested in that mystery. "Well, I did but apparently they don't exactly know what they are either." Laroxiam answered as he shook his head. Emily's excited expression quickly subsided as she began to think again. "Hey, Laroxiam, do you remember reading that book by any chance?" They inquired as Emily seemed lost in thought. "Now that you mention it, no. The only thing that I remember is the picture on the first page." Laroxiam responded after thinking for a few seconds.

"Huh, what are you guys talking about?" Emily asked after she began paying attention once again. "I had trouble sleeping last night, it felt like something or someone was keeping me awake so I just read a book that had a picture of a girl in a snowy forest with a weird looking sword in her hand. That's all I remember about it, unfortunately." Laroxiam explained which seemed to grab Emily's attention. "Oh, you're reading that book too? That story was always one of my favourites." Emily stated as a big smile formed across her face. "Yeah, I'm more into non-fictional stories though so it's really not my thing." Laroxiam spoke as Emily's smile really seemed to lighten his mood. Emily just looked at Laroxiam in confusion as if he didn't understand something.

"What's with that look that you're giving me?" Laroxiam asked as he stared back at her. They also seemed incredibly interested in what Emily was thinking about, almost as if that they had already figured it out. "Laroxiam, have you really been in this state of being ignored for that long?" Emily inquired as her face and her tone implied that she was feeling sympathetic. "What do you mean?" Laroxiam simply questioned her. "Well, most people only really learn about this in their teenage years... but from what you've told me, you must have been about ten years old when this whole thing started, right?" Emily seemingly thought out loud to herself. "Can you just get to the point? Laroxiam is feeling quite stressed from all of the mysteries, can you at least answer this one?" They requested after a sigh.

"Well, the thing is, that story isn't fictional. People do wield weapons like that even in the present day." Emily explained as she took a small blue orb out of her pocket. "I guess that's not totally unbelievable... but why did you hesitate to tell me something like that?" Laroxiam asked as Emily's answers were just confusing him more. "Laroxiam, you're so clueless. I guess I can't blame you though, if nobody is paying attention to you then I guess that you can't really learn anything." Emily stated as she began throwing the blue orb into the air and then catching it in her hand again. "Just give him a straight answer, damnit!" They yelled suddenly which shocked Emily a bit. "Seriously dude, calm down. I was about to get to that part." Emily spoke in a completely calm tone.

"You see, this may sound a bit unbelievable but I promise that it's the truth.

The thing is, the sword that the girl in the picture was holding is a weapon that is created from manifesting the life force within a person into a physical form." Emily stated as she looked at Laroxiam with a completely unwavering stare. Laroxiam stared back at her with suspicion and doubt before she continued speaking. "Those weapons vary from person to person as it depends on what they value most, what their goals in life are and more importantly, how malicious the wielder is. These different forms also vary in strength." Emily explained more thoroughly without the seriousness in her eyes fading for even a split second. Who would ever believe such an obviously fake story? One thing was for certain, Laroxiam definitely knew that it was fake and so he glanced over at them who looked back before nodding at him.

"That's a very interesting piece of information, Emily. Now, if all of what you've just said is true, then would you mind telling me why I haven't seen one of these weapons anywhere?" Laroxiam asked as he was completely convinced that Emily was lying to his face. "Well, for one, nobody has had a need to use them in centuries and also, to summon one of these weapons, you need to be really powerful when it comes to your will and life force and stuff like that. People nowadays have such an easy life to the point where their will and their desire to take the life force away from others has gradually subsided." Emily replied confidently. Laroxiam looked in their direction and they simply shook their head as if to tell him that it wasn't worth the trouble of continuing the conversation any longer. "Can you tell me when you're going to wake up from living in a world of fantasy? Sure, I can get the fact that you like a book that much but the fact that you're trying to make me believe that it's real is just disappointing honestly." Laroxiam stated before walking away with them.

Emily just looked at Laroxiam with complete shock at what he had just said as he walked away without a care in the world. After he had gotten a fair distance away from Emily, they started speaking to him. "What the hell was that? Do you really think that it's a good idea to talk like that to the only girl that can see you?" They asked in a tone that was clearly demonstrating just how irritated they were with Laroxiam. "Don't talk to me right now, for your own sake." Laroxiam replied without stopping. "This is the best thing that has happened to your life thus far and you're just going to insult her and walk away? What kind of moron are you?" They questioned whilst raising their voice ever higher. Laroxiam didn't speak another word, he just quickly turned around and began approaching them with burning rage in his eyes. They stared into the bright orange glow that was emanating from his eyes before they backed away.

Once they had increased the distance between the two of them, Laroxiam spoke once more. "Don't you think I already know that I messed up? Did you seriously think that I didn't regret saying that the moment the words left my mouth? What kind of heartless monster do you think I am?" Laroxiam asked as he stared them dead in the eyes. "I was born into a life where I'm just constantly forced to screw up everything in my life over and over again and yet the hope that I get every single time that something good comes into my life never fades no matter how many times I burn it to ashes! Emily is just another one of the good things that comes into my life and offers the hope that I so desperately desire just to rip it all away when I least expect it!" Laroxiam yelled before they even got a chance to respond to what he said last time.

"You of all people should understand this, you were the one who was constantly telling me that the outside world can only bring me pain and suffering. When did that all change for you? Was it when you met Emily? I thought you said that you were afraid of her!" Laroxiam shouted at the top of his lungs so that the whole world would hear him no matter how much it tried to ignore his existence. They couldn't respond after he spoke those words... all they could do was stare in shock and fear as the corrupted seed that would bring chaos had already been planted within Laroxiam's mind, it was now only a matter of time before it began to flower so brilliantly in the bright orange light. "What's with that orange glow in your eyes?" They asked when they saw a chance although they stuttered slightly which seemed to irritate Laroxiam even more. "It's the only thing that understands me, it is my only friend in this world that will constantly look out for me and keep me safe." Laroxiam stated before turning around and walking towards wherever his heart demanded to go.

"Look, Laroxiam, you don't understand what this world is like! If you carry on going down the road that you're travelling right now, then you'll become the very thing that you fear the most!" They yelled at Laroxiam as he ignored them and continued to travel the path that he had set for himself. There was nothing that could be done, no way to save him now, no words that could change his mind any longer. His fate was set in stone but even he didn't know what it was at the time. All Laroxiam knew was that the orange light that burned so brightly would be the very thing to let him know when he would have all of the information that he needed.

The voices that he could hear were blending together as they whispered their demands into his ear. "Keep going, you'll soon find everything that you're looking for. Don't let the others lead you astray." The voices demanded in such a soothing and calming way to the point where he couldn't resist their call. "I would never listen to them, I see what you're saying now, they're only making my life worse." Laroxiam agreed with the voices as he carried the fake sword with him. Eventually, the sounds became so distorted and quiet to the point where he couldn't understand them anymore. Suddenly, the voice of what seemed to be a teenage boy that was surprisingly deep whispered into his ear. "You know what you have to do, you just have to wake up first in order to realise your true potential." Was the last thing that was spoken to him in that moment.

After a few minutes of silence, Laroxiam blinked and his blind rage subsided and he realised what he had done. Laroxiam stopped moving and rested against a nearby wall before he thought about everything that he had said to Emily and them which caused him to cover his face in shame. Once he had spent a few minutes thinking about what he had done, he decided to try and set things right. "Hey, are you there? I'm not going to yell at you again, I swear." Laroxiam spoke in a quiet voice as he was so embarassed because of his own actions. "Apology accepted." They stated as they suddenly appeared behind him. "I didn't even say anything yet." Laroxiam said as he looked at them whilst avoiding eye contact. "Well, I shouted at you and you forgave me really quickly so I only thought tht it would be right to return the favour. Don't worry about it, seriously." They insisted which lightened the stress off of Laroxiam's shoulders slightly.

"What was happening to you? I heard you speaking to somebody but I didn't hear anybody else speaking." They curiously asked. "I think I was just hallucinating or something... or maybe I was just hearing things, I don't know, I can't really remember." Laroxiam replied with uncertainty. "Regardless, you need to go back there and apologise to her. You can't just let your life fall into ruin because of one accident." They stated as they only seemed to be looking out for Laroxiam. "You're right, it would be for the best for me if I went back there and tried to fix what I just did... but what about what's best for you? From what I can remember, you told me that Emily scares you... and I don't want to do what's best for me if it means that you have to constantly live in fear." Laroxiam conveyed as he seemed to be at a crossroads in his mind.

"Don't worry about me, I'll be gone the second that your life of negativity ends. I'm here just to make sure that you can escape your sadness and fear, nothing more." They explained in a completely calm tone. Laroxiam had to pause for a second to process what they had just told him. "What do you mean by that? People can't just disappear that simply." Laroxiam stated as he looked at them in confusion. "Well, normally people can't disappear at all but me and Emily do it all of the time, how do you explain that?" They asked. "I don't know, how do the two of you do that anyways?" Laroxiam answered with another question. "I wish I knew, it just sort of happens whenever I want it to." They replied with yet another shrug of their shoulders. "Maybe all of that fictional stuff that Emily talks about is actually true? It would explain quite a lot of the weird stuff that's happening now that I think about it." Laroxiam thought out loud.

"Maybe so but you're not going to find out by just standing here, go back and apologise already." They requested as they began to walk in the direction of where Laroxiam left Emily. "Wouldn't it be a bit awkward to go back right now? I feel like Emily would be more uncomfortable in that situation. Why don't we go back tomorrow?" Laroxiam suggested. "Yeah, you're probably right... but where else are we going to go for the rest of the day?" They asked after walking back to Laroxiam. "We'll figure it out." Laroxiam spoke as he began to take a stroll down a street that he had never previously visited. This path was different from all of the rest that Laroxiam had travelled, the buildings were all the same, that fact would never change no matter where he went but this was the only road that he had found that went up a hill.

"Hey, you never know, if you travel up this path, you could find some kind of legendary sword at the top or a ferocious beast of pure darkness." They spoke in a sarcastic voice which caused Laroxiam to chuckle a bit. "Come on, I was serious when I said that Emily could be telling the truth about all of that stuff that sounds like fantasy." Laroxiam responded as he reached the top of the hill. At the very top, Laroxiam found himself looking over a huge open field with bright green grass and nobody around. "Well, this is the first beautiful thing that I've seen in this world." Laroxiam admitted as he treaded lightly on the ground so he didn't ruin it accidentally. "Here comes the part where a mythical fairy descends from the heavens and grants you a special gift to slay the darkness with." They sarcastically stated. "Oh, just stop." Laroxiam said whilst trying to hold in his laughter.

After a moment of silence, Laroxiam began to rub his eyes and yawn. "This seems like the best place I'm going to find where I can have a peaceful sleep." Laroxiam stated as he sat down in the open field. "Are you kidding me? You literally just woke up!" They exclaimed as Laroxiam put his hood up before resting his head against the grass. "I went to sleep really late at night and I was woken up incredibly early and you expect me to not be tired? Just let me have a few more hours." Laroxiam requested as he slowly closed his eyes. "Fine, I'll let you have them this time but don't be mad at me if you can't go to sleep tomorrow." They replied as they sat down beside him. "You sound like an overprotective parent." Laroxiam simply said with a laugh as he began to drift off.

This time, Laroxiam's sleep was far from all of the others that he had previously. He felt completely conscious as he drifted about in the darkness. There was also an unnerving presence that he could sense that was watching him from afar... was that a feeling of chaotic intent that he could feel crawling up his arm? His arm felt completely frozen as whatever being was there with him clawed at his skin relentlessly as he felt its breath against his ear. "What the hell are you?" Laroxiam asked with his quivering voice.

There was no immediate response, instead Laroxiam's body felt like it was being enveloped by the same chilling presence that the sunlight in the outside world was constantly emitting. "I'm nothing and I am everything all at the same time. You, of all people, should know that." The presence explained in that same voice of the young boy that Laroxiam had heard earlier in the day. "Give me a straight answer!" Laroxiam demanded as his limbs felt like they might freeze completely any second.

"You want a straight answer that badly even though it would ruin everything about you? You're not ready to hear the truth of what I am." The voice replied which only frustrated Laroxiam more. "I'm tired of leaving these damn mysteries unsolved, I don't care if it ruins everything about me, just tell me the truth!" Laroxiam yelled as his entire body began to feel numb. "If you desire the truth so much, then I shall give it to you." The voice answered as Laroxiam's body suddenly began to feel a sharp consistent pain as if he was burning. "You are me but I am not you. That is the only answer that I can give you that won't break that fragile little mind of yours." The voice explained before the feeling of pain completely faded from Laroxiam's body.

Suddenly, the lucid dream that Laroxiam was having quickly faded as he returned back to a state of complete unconsciousness. That's when he saw that bright orange glow again... he did have to wonder whether it was giving him a choice or not. When he reached out for the light last time, it made him awaken once more... but what would happen if he ignored the ever so tempting call that he could hear as he stared directly at the source of the glowing? No, he couldn't just do that to the friend that understood him the most, they had so much in common and he was already having thoughts of ignoring their presence like the rest of the world does. "Nice to see you again, friend. It feels like we haven't spoken in years." Laroxiam stated as he reached out towards the light yet again.

All that Laroxiam could hear in response was two people laughing as if to agree with him. The voices sounded like the teenage boy that he had heard earlier along with a female that sounded vaguely similar to Emily. "There's two of you? Who are you both?" Laroxiam asked as he stared longingly into the bright orange light. There was no response to his question, all he could hear at that moment was the sound of a flame crackling from right in front of him. He could feel a tear falling down from his eye as if he had remembered something that he treasured for a long time. "Why... why did you have to do this to us?" Laroxiam inquired as he heard the male voice sniffling in the distance. "You all deserve to be your own people, it just... had to happen this way for you to get the lives that you wanted." The male voice answered with a wavering voice.

Everything suddenly went quiet after that before Laroxiam felt his eyes opening once again. Would he forget everything that he was thinking about at that moment if he woke up? "You want us to live the lives that we want to live? Well I'm stuck like this because of your wishes. I will find some way to break out of this hell and when I do, I can't promise that the others will be safe!" Laroxiam yelled just as the light of day shone upon his face once more.

"I was right about Laroxiam, he scares me whenever he talks. Whenever I look at him... no, whenever I so much as think about him, I cannot help but see a physical manifestation of what I fear that I'll become."

Chapter 5: "Mysteries"

"I know that heavy sleepers exist but this is just ridiculous." Laroxiam heard Emily say as he began to wake up. "Stop complaining, I'm awake now." Laroxiam spoke as he sat up in the field. Emily grabbed Laroxiam and looked him dead in the eyes. "Would you care to explain that conversation that you just had or are you going to force me to guess what's happening?" Emily asked in a stern voice. "What are you talking about? Can you loosen your grip a tiny bit? You're crushing my shoulder." Laroxiam stated before Emily shook her head let go of him. "Are you sure that you're alright?" They inquired as they knelt down beside him. "Why wouldn't I be?" Laroxiam answered with another question.

"You've been asleep for days, Laroxiam." Emily interjected before they could explain. "Yeah, sure I have. If I've been asleep for that long, then how come I haven't died of starvation or anything like that?" Laroxiam asked with a laugh as Emily was clearly joking once again. "Don't pretend like you don't know what's happening! I heard you speaking to those people in your sleep, you're clearly involved in this whole situation in some way!" Emily suddenly yelled which silenced Laroxiam. "Look, I remember having a conversation with something in my head but I don't remember the context behind all of what I said, I swear it!" Laroxiam explained to try and defend himself. "How did you even hear what I was saying?" Laroxiam questioned Emily before she had a chance to respond.

"You were speaking out loud the whole time, you can ask your invisible friend to confirm that if you don't believe me." Emily stated. Laroxiam looked back at them before they suddenly jumped at their sudden involvement of the conversation. "Yeah, you were talking in your sleep." They quickly said whilst nodding nervously. "Oh, Emily, about what happened yesterday, I'm sorry. I didn't mean anything that I said, I swear." Laroxiam apologised before he completely forgot to do it later. "I'll accept that apology only if you listen to what I have to say from this point onwards." Emily spoke in a slightly more calm tone. "Okay, I promise." Laroxiam responded as he slowly stood up before looking over to Emily.

Emily looked at Laroxiam with a completely serious expression before she began to speak again. "I'll just get straight to the point, something is happening and I don't know what." Emily stated which caught Laroxiam's attention. "You don't say." Laroxiam replied with a sarcastic voice. Emily just glared at Laroxiam which caused him to immediately shut up and continue listening. "People are ignoring me much like they are with you and they seem to be doing it exactly how you described it happening, they seem to be doing it because it's a natural instinct rather than a choice." Emily clarified which caused Laroxiam's eyes to widen. "You think that something is causing all of this, don't you?" Laroxiam asked as he had a sudden realisation. "Yes, there's no way that this is natural, I come into contact with you for a few days and suddenly, what happened to you a few years ago is now happening to me. I refuse to believe that this is all coincidental... how can all of this even be a coincidence?" Emily seemed like she was asking herself that question.

"Do you think it has anything to do with that story that we talked about yesterday?" Laroxiam asked as he was just throwing random questions about in the hopes that it would help. "Possibly, I'm not certain for myself so maybe it would be a good idea for me to read through it once more." Emily replied as she began to walk away. "Wait just one second! You need to explain this stuff to me before you just go and leave like that!" Laroxiam exclaimed as he quickly grabbed Emily's arm. "What is there to explain that you don't already understand?" Emily questioned Laroxiam without turning to face him. "There's only one thing that I want to know, why is that story so important to you? What does it say?" Laroxiam practically begged for an answer as his stress was growing from having too many unanswered questions.

"Are you actually willing to listen to what I'll have to say about it no matter how unrealistic it may sound?" Emily asked as she slowly turned back to face Laroxiam. Laroxiam nodded before letting go of Emily's arm and standing straight. "You'd better listen well then. The girl in the picture was a princess who lead the original civilisation of this world, she was the one who discovered how to create weapons using the life force that is held within." Emily explained partially. "I still find that hard to believe but... please continue." Laroxiam requested as he prepared himself to hear things that he were convinced weren't real. "There is a specific way to summon forth a weapon like that; you need to steal the life force of other beings and then you must feel an extreme form of any emotion. Once all that is done, the weapon supposedly just manifests in your hand." Emily seemed to read the instructions word for word from her memory. "I remember that you told me before that nobody can use those weapons anymore because their wills are weakened from not having to hunt or something like that, right?" Laroxiam repeated what he had already been told.

"From what I've read, that does seem to be the case." Emily confirmed what Laroxiam had just said. "When was the last time that those weapons were actually used in battle?" Laroxiam asked out of genuine curiosity. "Never." Emily bluntly stated. "Wait, what do you mean by that? How can you just forge a weapon made from the essence of life itself and then never use it for anything?" Laroxiam questioned Emily. "In every single history book that I've read, there has not been mention of a single act of violence at any point in time. Not a single one." Emily explained as she shook her own head as if she didn't believe it herself. "That doesn't make sense! How can the concept of violence itself even exist if it's never happened? Why is it even a word if the very thing that it's describing has never existed?" Laroxiam seemed to demand an answer from the very world itself as it was clear that Emily had no idea.

"Do you see why I've only just realised that everything is becoming strange? There were never any wars, no battle and no violence, so why do these things exist as concepts and ideas in the minds of normal people if those things never really happened?" Emily asked as she was clearly at a loss for what to think anymore. "There's something that I don't understand though; if people could use their life force to summon weapons, couldn't they have just used that same power to create other things?" Laroxiam inquired as Emily clearly knew more about the subject than he did. "Well, the people of that time believed that if they collected enough life energy from other living beings, then they'd be able to have the ability to create anything they wanted out of nothing by just snapping their fingers. Although, that's only what they assumed would happen, they never tested that theory for themselves as far as I can tell." Emily responded as she seemed to have not pondered that specific topic much for herself.

"Well, I don't see why they wouldn't have tried it." Laroxiam stated as he stared up into the beautiful blue sky. "They didn't try it because they would've had to kill every single creature on the planet along with about ninety percent of their own species to even get close to the amount that they guessed that they needed and all of that work clearly wasn't worth it." Emily explained as she turned to face Laroxiam. "Y-you'd really need to destroy that much just to be able to create whatever you wanted?" Laroxiam rhetorically asked in complete disbelief. "I've also read that there were supposedly powers that were beyond that such as the ability to possess others and even completely taking control of somebody else just by touching them." Emily responded as she continued to list of the terrifying possibilities of mankind.

"There's no way that any of that is real, right?" Laroxiam asked as he couldn't believe what Emily was stating was possible. "Well, considering the fact that the memories of us ever existing are being erased from the minds of others, I have reason to believe that somebody may have already achieved these powers and maybe even more beyond that." Emily spoke with a voice that sounded devoid of courage or determination... as if she'd already accepted her fate. "You've got to be joking, right? Please tell me that you're just messing around!" Laroxiam demanded after a moment of silence as he tried to comprehend the possibility of one person being in control of the minds of everybody else. "Well, I'm not joking but I'm also not one hundred percent sure that somebody has obtained that power. If they have, then I don't see how it's possible that this many people are still alive as from what I've read, you can create a body with that kind of power but you shouldn't be able to create a will nor a soul. It's either that or everybody in this world is fa-" Emily stopped herself from even uttering that last word. "What was that? I didn't quite catch that last part." Laroxiam stated as he looked at Emily who appeared to have so much fear and confusion in her eyes. Emily just seemed to contemplate what she was about to say before she attempted to put on as much of a brave face as she could before facing Laroxiam again. "I was meaning to give this to you, so that we could write about our own journeys after we find a way out of this mess." Emily explained as she handed Laroxiam what seemed to be a journal with a pen inside of it. "Emily, tell me what's wrong." Laroxiam insisted as he got slightly closer to her. She seemed to hesitate for a moment before Emily brought out the blue orb that she had the last time that Laroxiam saw her.

"I... I'm going to put an end to whoever is doing this and I'm going to start figuring this all out tonight." Emily said with an incredibly convincing confident tone in her voice... it only hurt Laroxiam more when he realised that Emily wasn't as sure about her decision as she was letting on.

"Let me help you." Laroxiam simply told Emily even though in his mind, he sounded more like he was pleading with her, begging her not to leave. Emily looked into Laroxiam's eyes before quickly looking away as he witnessed a tear roll down her face. "You don't need to be wrapped up in all of this, you just deserve to have a happy life. Besides, if both of us die whilst trying to stop this all powerful being then who's going to benefit from the life that it will bring?" Emily asked which seemed to confuse Laroxiam. "The billions of other people who live in this world will benefit from our success even if we die." Laroxiam stated with more confidence than Emily clearly had in herself. "You don't understand, nobody will live a happier life if we both die because... well, I just need you to know one thing." Emily replied without finishing her initial thought. "The people who live in this world are full of nothing but positivity, not that it really matters." Emily continued without giving Laroxiam a chance to respond.

"Emily, I'm not going to let you do this alone." Laroxiam stated as he stared directly into Emily's eyes with unwavering bravery. "You just don't get it, whenever the princess in that story did anything, she always did it by herself." Emily spoke whilst attempting to avoid eye contact with Laroxiam. "Why does that mean you have to do the same? You're not that princess, from what I've heard, you're no where near as powerful as she was. Doing this alone without those powers is a death wish." Laroxiam conveyed as he was now undeniably worried for Emily. Suddenly, Emily stopped holding back her emotions as her tears emerged from her eyes faster than they were before. "I wish that I was like that princess, that's why I have to do this alone." Emily replied as she clutched the orb in her hand tighter than ever before.

"Emily... I-" Laroxiam began to say as he reached out towards Emily... but then he blinked and she was gone just like before. For a moment, Laroxiam just stood completely still, as if he was frozen in time. "What now?" Was the only question that he could ask himself as he stood like a statue and stared at the empty space that was once occupied by his one and only friend. Laroxiam slowly pulled his hand back towards his body as the sudden realisation of what had just happened hit him straight in the face. "Why were you so determined to make those your last words? What information am I even supposed to get from "People only feel positivity, not that it matters." that doesn't even relate at all to the conversation that we were having." Laroxiam stated as he started feel his own sense of loss looming over his head.

"I wouldn't mourn just yet if I were you." They suddenly stated as they approached Laroxiam. "Give me one good reason why I shouldn't mourn when she's just gone to stop a presumably indestructible being." Laroxiam said with a sigh as he tried to hold back his tears. "Why do you think she gave you that journal? Emily knows that she's coming back and she just wants to be able to catch up with you quicker when she returns." They explained as they put their hand on Laroxiam's shoulder. "I... I guess so, there's also the possibility that we're just wrong in assuming that there's some kind of mastermind behind all of this so she could be in no danger at all for all we know." Laroxiam spoke in a pathetic attempt to convince himself that everything was better than it seemed.

"Listen to me, stop trying to lie to yourself. I'm just saying, we should stop panicking and give Emily a few weeks before we start worrying about her. Like you said, there's a very high probability that this guy that she's looking for doesn't even exist." They stated rather quickly to try to convince Laroxiam that everything was fine as they placed a hand on his shoulder. Laroxiam just stopped his current train of thought before he tried to figure out what Emily was trying to tell him. "People in this world are filled with nothing but positivity... not that it matters." Laroxiam repeated to himself as he was sure that there was some kind of hidden meaning behind Emily's words.

There was nothing that he could do at that moment except wait for Emily's return... if she ever returned. "So, what are we going to do?" They asked after letting go of Laroxiam. "What can we do now? Are we just supposed to go back to the life that we were living before we met her?" Laroxiam questioned himself mostly as he doubted that they would have an answer that either of them wanted. "Well, we should do what Emily asked us to do, write down our experiences and maybe even try to decipher what she meant by those last words of hers." They suggested as they were just throwing about ideas so that Laroxiam wouldn't be overwhelmed with stress.

"I guess you're right, I don't know how I didn't think that about you already though, you've proven that you know how the outside world works more than I do." Laroxiam stated as he opened the journal to find all of the pages blank and a single half-empty black pen. "Let's hang out somewhere where she'll be able to find us every single day, like the park for instance." They suggested as the two of them began to walk back to the familiar streets where the memories of Emily resided. As the two of them walked side by side back to the one place where his happiness had sprung from, Laroxiam began to write in the journal that Emily had given him.

"Day 1 Without you;

So, you've just handed me this journal that you're (hopefully) reading right now and I'm going to be writing down what happens everyday just like you asked me to. Our invisible friend says that you did this because you want to be able to read everything that I've done whilst you've been away... I guess that makes sense but I can't stop worrying about you. I'll keep writing just in case anything interesting happens but if there's nothing else here, just assume that today was just like all of the other days where you weren't present. I miss you already, I hope that you won't be gone for long but they've told me that you'll most likely be gone for a few weeks at the very least." Laroxiam read his thoughts out loud as he wrote them down.

"You don't have to sound so pessimistic when you're writing you know, wouldn't Emily want to know that you've had a great time and that she didn't upset you by leaving?" They asked as they seemed to be concerned for no reason whatsoever. "No, I think she would like to hear the truth more than anything." Laroxiam replied as he looked down at the journal. As the two of them began to walk back to the park where they intended to wait for Emily's arrival, Laroxiam looked at his surroundings once more in the hopes that he would find something different. All the people that he passed on the street had that same stupid smile that started to look more like a mask that they were wearing over their faces, their body language seemed to imply that they were all way more joyful than what seemed natural.

"You know, I'm starting to see what Emily was saying. None of these people would benefit from a change to this world where we beat whoever this guy is that's hiding away but we both die in the end... they'd all just be blissfully ignorant of whatever changes that we would bring." Laroxiam stated as he continued to walk back down the hill. "I've also noticed what she meant by "Everybody in this world is full of only positivity." They're all just smiling even though there are people like you who are just suffering." They agreed with Laroxiam as the two of them reached the bottom of the hill. "I still don't get what she meant by that. If what she said about everybody being positive and never negative, how do you explain what happened to Oliver? I don't know about you but Oliver didn't really seem all too positive when we saw him." Laroxiam stated as he turned to the bright, green grass that he had grown to love.

"I'm sure that Emily will answer all of our questions when she comes back so I'd just save all of what you have to ask until then, she's really good with figuring this type of stuff out, wouldn't you agree?" They asked as they rested themselves against a nearby tree. "Yeah, I'm sure that when Emily comes back, everything will be fine. This mastermind will be gone, people will start being able to see me again and we'll all start living a life which we can be proud of." Laroxiam agreed as he closed his eyes and imagined a world where nothing went wrong. Never-ending peace and tranquility which would be comparable to that which he experiences in his dream... that was all that he wished for in that world.

Little did he know, the end was quickly approaching, nothing would ever last as long as he wanted it to.

"'You wish you were.' Is that what you said?"

Chapter 6: "Bargaining"

"Day 2 Without you;

Nothing much has changed, we're just sat here, waiting for you to return. The fifth of July is when I started writing this, even if I can't find a calender, at least I'll know what date it is just by writing my notes down. I've just been thinking, should I be training myself just in case the worst happens to you? Maybe if you fail, then I'll be able to continue where you left off. They keep telling me that I shouldn't be constantly thinking of every worst-case scenario but I just can't help myself when it comes to the situation that we're in now. I know that what you're doing is important but we keep telling each other that we'd give up everything we had just so we could see you again. I miss you."

"Day 3 Without you;

We both agreed that I should be training just in case you don't return. Thankfully, I have a fake sword that I can practice with although I don't really have any targets that act enough like people to use it on. I've also noticed that if I do need to take your place to try and save this world, I don't have any actual weapons that I could use. Maybe I could find some alternate way to summon one of those life force weapons that you mentioned? I really do wish that you'd come back soon. I miss you."

"Day 4 Without you;

I went back to the house where I first read that book to thankfully find that it was still there and in the same position as I last left it. We're going to be reading through it until you come back and maybe then we'll actually be prepared for what is to come... that is, if anything actually ends up happening. I've only just started training with my sword but I already feel like I'm getting pretty good at it so if you ever need my help, I'll be ready. There's something interesting that I noticed about the princess in the picture at the beginning of that book; you know how you mentioned that she ruled over the first ever civilisation in this world? Well, I just noticed that she's wearing rather modern looking clothes like a hoodie and stuff like that. Did you notice that too? I miss you."

"Day 5 Without you;
Wow, you could've told us how awesome some of these weapons looked! I've noticed how a lot of those weapons are blades that can transform into ranged weapons, I can't believe that these types of things actually existed! Although, I guess that they do harness the power of life itself and when I think about that, the possibilities seem almost endless for these things! If I find some way to wield one of those things, then I think that we'll be able to beat this mastermind without any problems! Regardless of all of that, I've noticed that you've been gone for almost a week now without showing up to at least tell me that you're alright. I know that you're probably fine and that you're just focusing really hard on tracking this guy down but... I don't know, I can't help but worry about you. I miss you.

"Day 6 Without you;
Did you read that book all of the way through? I'm just wondering because I skipped past some of the writing that was just telling the tale of the princess and I heard about something that I don't remember you mentioning. They call them "Dark Spirits" or "Shadows". They're something like demons that supposedly take advantage over people with a damaged mental state. At first, I thought that our invisible friend may be one of them but the Shadows are constantly described as aggressive creatures that don't hesitate

to lash out on their victims. They clearly haven't done anything like that and I've been with them for nearly four years by this point. Let's discuss this when you come back from your journey. I miss you."

"Day 7 Without you;
It's times like these where I think about what happened to Oliver. Why did he react like that? I get the feeling that you already know that answer but it's just that you want me to figure it out for myself. Does it have something to do with what you said on the last day that I saw you? "People are only filled with positivity and nothing else." Or something like that, right? I've been trying to figure out what that means but every conclusion that I come to is either completely contradicted by something that I already know or it just flat out doesn't make sense. This mystery is going to need your immense knowledge to be solved. I miss you."

"Day 8 Without you;
So, I've just remembered something that they told me but you weren't there to hear it; they told me that they would disappear when I finally have a positive life. I don't know what they mean by that, it's like they've convinced themselves that my negative life is somehow tied to their very existence. They seemed to have lightened up recently though, so I think that they're finally understanding that their life matters too. The last time we spoke before we met up with you again, they almost seemed depressed... although, I'll be honest, I have never seen a depressed person so I wouldn't know for definite. I've read through the book a bit more but I can't find any information on if you can summon a weapon like those you mentioned without stealing the life from others. I hope that we'll be able to figure it out together. I miss you."

"Day ???

Well, I finally lost track of the days. Me and our friend spent a few days of practice and I completely forgot to write in the journal. Until I find a calender, I won't be sure of how many days have passed. By the way, I can't find any information in that book about any of the other powers that life force grants according to you. Are you sure that you're not just mixing up two completely seperate stories? I'm starting to get worried for you... like, a lot more than before. Please come back soon. I miss you."

"Day ???

I think that we're as prepared as we're ever going to be. All that's left to do now is to wait for you to come back. I've been thinking, should we try and steal life force from other creatures... you know, only as a last resort just in case. Of course, I'd only really want to do that plan if we had literally no other option. There's too much time in our hands and all we're doing with it is waiting for you to come back. Could you speed up your plan a bit? We really want to see your face again. I miss you."

"Day 37

Well, as we were investigating another house, we found a calender so I was able to find out how long we had spent without you. I'll be honest, I'm really starting to lose hope here, I can tell that they're feeling the same way. Our mentalities are suffering from all of the stress and there's one thing that would just fix all of that in an instant; you returning to us. I miss you more than you could ever know.

"Day 54

You're not coming back, are you?"

"Day 73

If you can only steal the life force from a living creature that you've killed, that means that nobody should have any more life force than they normally have because nobody has been reported as missing or dead. There is supposedly a mastermind behind all of this that Emily is after who has the powers that the old book spoke of. How can there be a mastermind with that much power if nobody has ever died? The only logical answer is that this 'mastermind' doesn't actually exist and that Emily just made it up. Why would Emily lie to me about something like that? She must have gone mad, right?"

"Day 89

Nothing makes sense anymore, Emily's last words just confuse me even more than the people do. "People in this world are full of nothing but positivity." What a bunch of nonsense. Yet still, even though she lied to me, everything seems to be conspiring to push me further and further down the path that I wish to tread. Emily, please come back, I'm not angry, I just want some explanations."

"Day 118

I think that I'll... we-" Laroxiam began writing before he just dropped the journal to the floor and the pen along with it. "I can't do this anymore." Laroxiam stated as he began crying into his hands. "You can't give up now, you need to keep going, if you don't, then just imagine how disappointed Emily would be." They spoke to attempt to convince Laroxiam to persist through his life. "I don't give a damn about Emily anymore! She's lied to me about so much to the point where I just can't care!" Laroxiam exclaimed as the tears streamed down his face. "You don't believe that." They simply replied as they shook their head. "You're right, I don't... but I'm going to keep shouting it until my mind accepts it as the truth." Laroxiam explained as he folded his arms and tightened his grip.

"Ever since she entered my life, everything became so much easier but that came with so much confusion. I don't know if I would've prefered it if I continued my life without seeing her at all." Laroxiam conveyed as he felt powerless in the current situation so he just dwelled on everything that happened in the past and what could've been. "Listen to me, you need to stop doing this, you need to carry on for Emily. We both know that she isn't coming back, there's nothing that we can do nor was there anything that we could've done to prevent this from happening. Emily made up her mind and now you have a choice. You can either continue on down the path that she's travelled or you can accept the life that has been forced upon you." They stated with a strong and confident voice.

"I'm tired of you and Emily just forcing these expectations onto me... why can't I just have a life that I can live by myself without others judging me or constantly expecting me to do something?" Laroxiam rhetorically asked as his eyelids began to feel heavier than ever before. "We're not expecting you to do anything, you brought these expectations on yourself. Emily only wanted you to sit back and live a happy life whilst she went out and did all of the hard work." They stated in a such a calm manner that seemed to irritate Laroxiam. "Why did you constantly tell me to avoid the outside world and then, all of a sudden, you just wanted me to spend more time with Emily in that same place?" Laroxiam inquired as he just wanted some of the questions that had been unanswered to finally be made clear. "I... I just wanted to protect you. This world brought you nothing but suffering back when I used to tell you to stay at home. When you met Emily, I saw that you didn't need me to keep you safe anymore and so I just wanted you to be with her and be happy." They explained with a quieter voice than normal.

"You... wanted to protect me? That's the only reason why you said all of that?" Laroxiam asked in a sudden moment of realisation. "The only reason." They replied which made Laroxiam feel worse about himself. "I thought that you were making fun of me. It always sounded like you were trying to drag me down whenever I was having a good time." Laroxiam stated as he looked back on all of the moments like that which he could remember only to realise that the words that they said could've been taken a different way... a different way that he always ignored. "Did I really make you feel that way? I'm so sorry, I didn't mean that at all. Just making me think about how I've been saying stuff like that for a few years now and you've always thought that I was insulting you or something like that, it makes me sick just imagining having to put up with that." They explained as they seemed to have that same moment of comprehension.

The two of them remained silent as they thought back on moments where they made mistakes when talking to each other before Laroxiam spoke up once again. "So, why did you feel like you had to protect me? Literally nobody besides from Emily ever even spoke to me." Laroxiam asked as he just felt like he needed to know every reason behind their actions. "You already know the answer to that question, Laroxiam." They replied as they didn't seem to want to give Laroxiam a straight answer. "Come on, I just want to get to know you better before we have to do something that I might regret. Can't you at least allow me to clear my mind of these questions that might not even matter?" Laroxiam requested as he was prepared for the worst to happen when he eventually attempted to follow in Emily's footsteps. They remained silent for a while as they seemed to contemplate whether or not telling Laroxiam what he wanted to know was the right thing to do.

"I'll be honest, I don't have all of the details right at this moment but I do know some things about myself that I think you'll want to know." They stated as they seemed to be stalling for time as they didn't want to divulge in the knowledge that Laroxiam specifically asked for. "Take your time, I'll wait for as long as it takes to hear what you have to say." Laroxiam said in an attempt to calm them slightly. "Saying that isn't helping, if anything, it just pressures me to tell you more." They explained as they seemed to be on edge. "Well, I'll just stay quiet then." Laroxiam replied before remaining silent as he waited for an answer to his previous question. After a few moments of deafening silence, they began speaking once again. "This isn't helping either, it just feels like you're silently judging me or something!" They exclaimed as the stress was practically killing them.

"Look, if you just tell me then you won't have anything to be pressured about." Laroxiam spoke to finally break his silence. "I guess that's true but... you of all people should know that it isn't that easy." They stated as they held their head. "Yeah, I really do understand that, it's like I'm talking to my reflection, in fact, I always felt like you knew exactly how I was thinking throughout all of the time that we've known each other." Laroxiam thought out loud which suddenly made their eyes open wide and their gaze suddenly shot up towards him. "Yes, that's exactly what I was trying to tell you!" They suddenly exclaimed before almost immediately looking away as if they regretted what they just said. Laroxiam paused his own train of thought as he processed what they had just told him. "You're a reflection of me, is that what you're trying to say?" Laroxiam asked as if he was finally beginning to understand.

"Well, I'm not exactly sure but there is a lot of evidence that points towards that conclusion." They explained as if even they weren't so sure about what they were saying. "No, that doesn't make sense. I've never even heard of something like that being real before, you're definitely not a dark spirit or a shadow that the book talks about... but then again, that book never mentioned anything that sounds even remotely like you in the slightest." Laroxiam stated as he thought back on everything that he had learned. "I think that I might have a reason as to why nothing like me has ever been mentioned before as well." They said as Laroxiam watched them visibly shiver at whatever they were thinking about. "Would you care to indulge me?" Laroxiam requested as he began to walk towards them. They looked up at him with fear in their eyes as they seemed to think about what they were about to say a little longer.

"I... I think that the reason that nothing that we've read has ever mentioned something like me is because a being like me has never existed before. In fact, I don't think a creature like me has ever existed... ever, not even right at this moment." They explained as they slowly clenched their fist at just the thought of what he was talking about. "Y-You don't mean-" Laroxiam was about to ask before he was interrupted. "What if I'm not real? What if I never was real?" They questioned their very existence with Laroxiam as a witness. "No, I won't accept that as the truth!" Laroxiam spoke way louder than necessary as he stared straight into their eyes. "Well, why not? The evidence is all there and you're actively choosing to deny it all for no reason?" They asked as their mentality seemed to be falling ever deeper down into a dark, empty space. Laroxiam began stuttering as he tried to come up with an answer that could discredit all of the evidence that they had presented only for him to fail to respond with anything.

Laroxiam stopped his thinking and decided that instead of trying to look for an answer in logic, he would find an answer in his emotions. "You know, you are just like me, Laroxiam. You're such a pessimist much like myself."

Laroxiam said with a laugh which just seemed to make their negative emotions grow. "Don't call me that. I'm not Laroxiam anymore, you deserve that name more than me." They insisted that their own identity didn't belong to them anymore. "We both deserve that name as much as each other. If we're the same then that means that you're just as real as me, right?" Laroxiam asked in an attempt to convince them. "No, that's not true, we're not the same. There's a reason why you took my name as your own without realising it and that's because you're meant to exist and I'm not. This world is slowly trying to remove me from existence and neither of us can stop it, it's for the best if we just let it happen." They replied dismissively.

"I won't accept that as the truth, the mastermind is just trying to make us lose hope so that we don't attack him, that's all." Laroxiam stated even though he didn't really believe his own words. "Are you even sure that this 'mastermind' is even real?" They asked as an attempt to stop Laroxiam from trying to convince them to change their mind. "That doesn't matter at this moment. Listen to me, it isn't just me that Emily wants to see when she comes back, she needs to see you as well." Laroxiam attempted to use Emily as an excuse for them to not lose hope. "She can't see me." They simply said as they were trying to point out any inaccuracies even if they didn't matter. "You know what I mean!" Laroxiam exclaimed as their complacent nature was irritating him. "I don't care what you mean, I would've given up my life at any point to bring Emily back just so that you could live a happy life with her!" They retorted without a second thought.

Laroxiam lowered his tone slightly and took a silent breath before replying. "I would've done the same thing for you if I was given the chance." Laroxiam stated with a completely serious expression which caused them to gasp and look up at Laroxiam in surprise. "How could you say something like that? You'd let a fake being like myself just take your place in this world if you were given the chance?" They asked in complete disbelief. "You're not fake, just listen to me for one second. I would gladly let somebody like you take my place and make this life a happy one if they so wished." Laroxiam explained again with the same dead serious face. They just stared at Laroxiam in complete confusion before they looked at the ground with a hint of disappointment in their eyes. "Well, it's pointless to continue talking about this if I can't convince you. Let's forget all about the whole thing where we say: "I'd sacrifice myself for you to live a happy life." Instead, I'll just say what we're both thinking. We'd both do anything just to bring Emily back, right?" They inquired even though they already knew the answer. "Anything." Laroxiam agreed before sighing and turning back to the swing that he was sat on previously. "I wonder, would she do the same for us?" They asked as they were just thinking out loud. "What kind of a question is that? Of course she would!" Laroxiam replied even though he was beginning to doubt if that was true as well. "How can you be so sure?" They questioned Laroxiam as it was clear that he wasn't being completely truthful about what he believed. "Well, I have enough proof that she would do that. That proof being that she literally sacrificed herself to allow us to live on. She was determined to let us live a happy life and that's why she left." Laroxiam said in an attempt to convince himself that Emily didn't leave just to get away from him.

"You know as much as I do that she must have been lying about what she was intending to accomplish by leaving us. She just knew that her life would be happier if we were not a part of it." They insisted on trying to convince Laroxiam that their distorted beliefs were the truth. Laroxiam just remained silent, the arguement that he was having seemed to just be repeating itself over and over again. "I know that we agreed that we were going to wait for Emily to come back before we did anything and that if she didn't come back today, we'd act immediately... but can wait at least one more day?" Laroxiam requested as he wasn't mentally prepared enough to enact the plan that the two of them had concocted. "I'd much prefer if we didn't go through with this at all but sure, why not? At least something interesting would happen." They agreed without giving a clear indication as to whether they completely agreed with the idea or not.

"I'm not doing this for my own amusement, we're going to do this so that we can defeat the mastermind and save Emily." Laroxiam reminded them as he used the most serious and intimidating voice that he could as he stared right into their eyes. They looked back into Laroxiam's eyes with the most blank stare that eseentially told him that they didn't believe a word that he said. "Well, I don't care why you're doing it, I'm going to have to watch, listen and feel whatever it is that you do. In fact, I've just thought of a little trick that we could work into our plan that would make your job a lot easier." They stated without changing their expression in the slightest. "That would be greatly appreciated." Laroxiam answered as he began to walk back home. "Well, if you're so convinced that we're exactly the same then you must think that we have the exact same amount of life force at all times, right? Just as an example, you think that if you take the life force from another living being that I'll also gain the same amount of life force, correct? What if, just in case things went wrong, I offered you the life force that sustains my existence if you're in a perilous situation?" They suggested which caused Laroxiam to freeze in place.

"No." Laroxiam simply spoke as he didn't even want to consider the idea. "You act like you'll have a choice if it ever gets to that point." They stated with a cold voice that chilled Laroxiam to his very core. "I don't care, I won't let you do that even if it means that I will die in the end!" Laroxiam exclaimed as he wasn't ready to see them reduced to nothing by their own decisions and be okay with it. "You're scared, aren't you? Although, you're not scared because you don't want to see your friend die, no. The reason you're scared is because I am exactly like you, you're afraid that you're going to see yourself die before you actually feel death for yourself." They explained what they believed that Laroxiam was thinking.

"No, you may be exactly like me but you're also the greatest friend that I've ever had in this world, I can't just agree with this plan of yours!" Laroxiam yelled to try to get the information into their head. "Say whatever you want, I know the truth and I've accepted it... and I willingly embrace it." They said before disappearing once more. Laroxiam's mind was filled with nothing but confusion and fear at that point as he stared up into the dark grey clouds that were gathering overhead. "Whoever you are, no matter the reasons that you have for doing this, I will bring you down." Laroxiam spoke with confidence as his muscles tensed at the idea of having to go along with the plan that he had for the day after the one that he was living through at that moment.

"Oh, you poor little thing, if only you had a choice in the matter."

Chapter 7: "Depression"

Thankfully, the peaceful darkness of sleep had returned instead of the unnerving voices and freezing temperatures. It seemed like this world decided to grant him one last good thing before everything was destined to fall down a never-ending hill of bad decisions and evil intent. He could finally feel it, in this endless nothingness, he had found his clarity, his determination, his will to carry on travelling down the path where nobody else had dared to go. The only thing that was missing from this perfect picture was that orange light that he related to so much... where was it? "If it's not here then I'll just make one that's similar enough." Laroxiam thought to himself and for once, the entire world seemed to agree with him. "Well, it's time to wake up, get up and get to work." Laroxiam told himself as he willingly abandoned the one thing that mattered the most to him in that moment just so he could do what he believed was right.

The second that Laroxiam woke up, he felt like he was full of energy and so he was out of bed within a few seconds which, when compared to the normal amount of minutes that he spent contemplating his own life in bed on practically all of the previous days, was quite impressive. They looked up at Laroxiam as he prepared for the most eventful day of his life. "It's now or never." Laroxiam stated as he stared back at them. Even though Laroxiam only got a nod in response to what he had just said, he felt as if that they had given him more than enough confirmation to go through with the plan. "First, we check if Emily has returned... and if she hasn't, then we'll do the entire thing with no regrets, agreed?" Laroxiam asked to just confirm that he was remembering everything correctly. "Agreed, it all ends today." They replied which caused Laroxiam to smile as he rushed downstairs and towards the front door.

He was almost completely placing his hopes on the fact that Emily would be waiting for him to arrive after everything that had happened. Laroxiam passed all of the identical buildings that lined the street that he couldn't even tell if they really existed or not before he made his way to the tall grass that blocked the only visible way to the park. After he pushed his way through the greenery, he closed his eyes and took a deep breath as he continued to traverse the pathway that he had memorised. The two of them stood before the swings that Laroxiam remembered loving so much... before he opened his eyes... and found nobody waiting there.

That was it, that was the breaking point. Laroxiam collapsed to the ground as he had finally come to the realisation of had happened to Emily... she wasn't coming back. They just remained silent as they watched Laroxiam fall to his hands and knees as his tears fell to the ground. "Why... why did it have to come to this?" Laroxiam asked anything that was listening in the hopes that he would get an answer that would leave him with no more questions. "Laroxiam, we should-" They began saying before being cut off. "I know, there's no turning back now. We need to stick to the plan, we have to carry on no matter what happens from this point onwards." Laroxiam stated as he slowly pushed himself away from the ground and back onto his own two feet.

"This needs to end, today." Laroxiam spoke as he wiped the tears away from his eyes and attempted to compose himself. "Don't hold anything back or you might never see another day." They added onto Laroxiam's original thought which made him nod at them before he turned back towards the entrance of the park. Suddenly, something caught Laroxiam's eye; it looked like a sheet of paper that was being held to the ground by a large stone. They seemed to notice the stone as well. "You don't think-" Laroxiam was about to ask before they cut him off. "Possibly, we won't know unless if you check, will we?" They rhetorically asked. With that, Laroxiam approached the piece of paper before he released it from beneath the rock and looked at what it said.

"Do not check on Oliver." Laroxiam read the note out loud as he examined the writing closely. The letters were red and they seemed to be painted on rather than written and the style of the letters seemed as if they were quickly placed there as if the person who made the message were in a rush. "Did Emily write this?" Laroxiam asked out loud as he examined the back of the paper only to find that there was nothing else written there. "That seems to be the most likely possibility... although I don't think it is the only conclusion that we can come to." They explained which made Laroxiam think about it for a bit longer. After a moment of considering his options, Laroxiam turned to them with a smile on his face. "If this was written by the mastermind that may or may not exist, then I should clearly do the opposite of what it says." Laroxiam conveyed his thoughts.

"What if the letter was written by Emily?" They asked as they wanted to understand how Laroxiam thought. "Well, then I'd say that we should go to Oliver's regardless of what she's warning me of. I asked her back in the day whether she'd be there if I ever needed her and she told me that she would. Here we are, when we both need her the most and she's nowhere to be found... if she's going to go against what we want then I say that we go against what she wants." Laroxiam explained his thinking process with confidence that he was right. "That doesn't make all that much sense." They stated as they shook their head. "You're trying to make sense of a world that doesn't care about how anybody thinks. Plus, you can't deny that it would be fun to reject everything that people tell us to do and just do our own thing for once." Laroxiam replied to them which seemed to make them agree with him... even if it was only a little bit.

"Fun? I thought that you told me yesterday that you weren't doing this for your own amusement." They reminded Laroxiam of what he had promised himself. "Well, that's the thing, this time, I'm doing it for your amusement since you're so convinced that you're going to fade away soon, I thought that I'd just let you have a bit more fun until it's time to say goodbye to this life." Laroxiam explained to them in the hopes that it would convince them to side with him. "Don't waste your time trying to bring joy to a useless fake creature like myself." They requested as Laroxiam began to take the same steps that he took when Emily first led him to Oliver's shop. "So, what is it that you plan to do when you get there or are you just stalling for time so that you don't have to go through with our original plan?" They inquired as they had convinced themselves that Laroxiam was doing everything that he could to avoid what he had promised to do.

"You know, I think I've figured out what Emily meant to tell me when she said that everybody in this world was filled with positivity and nothing else." Laroxiam stated as he ignored their previous question. "Oh, what would that be?" They asked as they seemed to find some enjoyment in having potential answers to some of the questions that had plagued their mind for an unbelievable amount of time. "I don't know for definite but I think I'm very close to figuring it out. Maybe if I ask Oliver a few questions about it, I'll be able to tell you." Laroxiam explained as he began approaching the familiar looking building that he recognised as Oliver's shop... although every building looked the same so the only way that he was able to tell that he was in the right place was thanks to the sign that was hanging over the door. Laroxiam stopped and calmed his thoughts as he approached the door and pulled the handle down... surprisingly, the door wasn't locked, in fact it wasn't even fully closed.

"Oliver, are you there? It's me, Laroxiam, I'm not here to hurt you, I just want to ask some questions." Laroxiam spoke out into the empty shop only to be met with no response. "Are you sure that he's even home?" They asked as Laroxiam began to look around at the barren walls and floor. "I can't know for definite until I check every single room... I'll start with the bedroom that should be upstairs if all of these houses truly are the same." Laroxiam stated as he spotted the stairs and began climbing them one step at a time. Suddenly, a chill shot down Laroxiam's spine that made him feel uneasy about what he was doing. He stopped after only having climbed five steps to try and gather his thoughts along with the courage that he required to carry on. "Remember what we said; no fear, no regrets." They repeated to Laroxiam which was only just enough to convince him to continue up the stairs albeit at a slower pace.

"I have to do this, no matter what happens afterwards, I need to see this through to the end." Laroxiam kept telling himself after each and every step. Before he knew it, Laroxiam was at the top of the stairs, he looked around only to realise that every single door was open except for one... the bedroom of which he was currently heading to investigate. "No fear, no regrets." Laroxiam repeated to himself as he reached out towards the door and felt the cold metal handle against his grip. Finally, after having to talk himself into continuing once again, Laroxiam slowly pushed the door open and peered inside. "Oliver, are you th-" Laroxiam began to ask before he stopped and quickly stepped backwards before tripping over and falling face-first onto the ground. As Laroxiam began to push himself back up, he imagined what he had seen in that room and he had to force himself to repress the urge to throw up which he nearly failed to accomplish.

After a moment of self-composure, Laroxiam stood up with his back to Oliver's bedroom. "What... the hell?" Laroxiam asked himself as he attempted to make sense of what he had seen. He looked around momentarilly to see that they had disappeared once again so he couldn't ask them to confirm what he had witnessed... the only choice that he had was to turn around once more and check for himself. Hesitantly, Laroxiam's feet shuffled around and he forced his gaze to the ground as he hadn't fully prepared himself.. not that it mattered; he could see the shadow stretching out towards him thanks to the light that was emerging from the window. At last, Laroxiam raised his head as he swallowed one last time and held his mouth shut as tight as he could.

Once his eyes had locked with the sight a second time, there was no way that Laroxiam could deny the truth. He looked inside of Oliver's room to see dark red writing and scribblings covering the walls that repeated the same phrases and words over and over. Things like "Negativity" or "What the hell is negativity?" All of these must have been written at least one hundred times each over each surface including the furniture and the ceiling. These thoughts that clearly came from the mind of a mad man were not grabbing Laroxiam's attention though. The things that Laroxiam was focused on the most... were a piece of rope that was hanging from the ceiling, a stool that had been knocked over just underneath it and a human-shaped object that was wearing the same clothes that Oliver wore on the last day that Laroxiam had seen him. He called it an object because that's what it was, it may have been filled with life at one point and maybe even more than one emotion... but it had no longer had either of those... it wasn't a person any longer.

Laroxiam also noticed that the clothes that it was wearing had been torn and that there were deep cuts around the stomach and on the hands. The part that sickened him the most was the face; it seemed completely fine, as if it had been untouched by whatever chaos had torn through the rest of the body. That smile... that damned smile that was plastered over everybody's faces also seemed to remain on Oliver until the end... in fact, it still remained even after the end. It was the one thing that every living being carried with them at all times and it defiled the body of this one poor soul who had taken his own life in an attempt to escape it. Everything became clear; the world had no shame and no honour, it would do whatever it wanted to anybody and all they could do is either sit there and accept it or force their way out of the world permanently.

Laroxiam stood and looked at the entire scene with that horrible feeling building in his gut once again. Time itself just seemed to freeze as he observed what happened to those who witnessed negativity firsthand. Nothing else mattered at that moment, every single negative emotion that Laroxiam could feel seemed to scratch and claw at his mind as each one attempted to take control of him for themselves. He was enraged at the world for allowing this to happen, he was afraid as he considered that the same thing could happen to himself in the future, disgusted because of the sight before him. In the end, he attempted to scream or shout to let the feelings that he had been containing for the past few years to be let free but he found himself unable to do anything but continue looking on in horror.

As if he simply flicked a switch, Laroxiam's emotions all suddenly left his mind and his attention turned to the writing on the walls. "Negativity." Laroxiam read aloud as he thought about everything that he had assumed about the world that he was in and if the information on the wall could help prove his theories right. He thought about what may have lead to this outcome. Oliver first started acting strange when he apparently saw Laroxiam for the first time and Emily mentioned negativity and when he escorted the two of them out of the shop, he began loudly weeping but everybody else who walked by seemed to not be able to hear it. "I feel like my theory is right." Laroxiam stated as he saw Oliver's body in the corner of his eye before quickly looking away. "Would you care to tell me about your theory then?" They requested as they suddenly appeared again.

"Emily mentioned how everybody is filled with positivity but for some reason, Oliver freaked out the second that he saw me. My theory is that the reason that everybody wears that same stupid smile is because they only feel positivity but did you notice that the second that Emily brought up negativity, Oliver questioned what she meant as if he had never heard of it before and then he saw me?" Laroxiam explained partially before stopping just so that they could comprehend what he was about to say. "Continue." They said after a moment of processing the information. "I think that the people in this world that are under the mastermind's control literally can't feel negativity and are unaware that negativity actually exists until somebody mentions it. Whenever anybody feels negative emotions, they become invisible and those people are unable to be heard." Laroxiam finished explaining. "That... does seem like a possibility but I don't see enough evidence to prove it." They stated as they seemed to seriously consider what Laroxiam had to say.

"I can get all of the prove that you need right now." Laroxiam spoke as he exited the room whilst covering his mouth so he wouldn't vomit if he got a glimpse inside of the room again. "Where are you going?" They asked as Laroxiam descended the stairs and walked out of the front door. "Just give me a second and I'll show you." Laroxiam explained as he took a few deep breaths of the fresh air before walking over to a nearby house and picking up a large stone along the way. "What are you-" They were about to ask before Laroxiam threw the rock as hard as he could at a large window of the nearest building only for the glass to shatter immediately. "What the hell are you doing!?" They questioned Laroxiam as he was surely going to get in trouble for his actions. "Watch." Laroxiam said as he looked at the people who were inside of the building... they didn't seem to pay attention at all. "You see, they ignore anything and everything that would normally cause a negative reaction from within them." Laroxiam stated as he walked into the building to observe the family closer. They simply stared in surprise as they were still confused as to how Laroxiam managed to figure all of this out. "This will make our job a lot easier." Laroxiam said as he made his way to the kitchen and opened the drawer that was filled with all of the sharpest knives as it was with every single house. "I see what you're saying, if they ignore everything that is related to negativity, then they'll ignore you if you kill somebody in front of them and they'll also most likely ignore the body as well, right?" They asked as they finally began to realise what Laroxiam was getting at. "Precisely." Laroxiam bluntly spoke before he walked over to a family that was gathering for some kind of meal; a father, a mother and their two children.

"There's only one thing that's holding me back now." Laroxiam stated as he looked down at his newly found weapon. "You're afraid that you're going to regret every single one of your decisions from this point onwards, right?" They asked sympathetically. "How did you know?" Laroxiam sarcastically inquired with a laugh as he stared at all of their happy faces that suddenly didn't seem so annoying anymore. "I know how you feel but you already swore to yourself that you wouldn't hold back anymore, no matter what happens." They reminded Laroxiam in an attempt to get him back on the path that fate had decided that he would walk. "Do you really think that I care about that anymore?" Laroxiam rhetorically questioned them as he leaned against the wall and held his head that began to hurt once again.

"If you go along with this, if you succeed, you'll be able to change this world for the better. You'll be doing them all a favour by releasing them from this corrupted world. You can bring them all back once you reach your end goal." They continued to list reasons as to why Laroxiam shouldn't give up at the point of no return. "You're not helping all that much, if anything, I'm just doubting myself more now." Laroxiam explained which made them rethink their strategy to attempt to convince him.

"Anything for Emily." They repeated Laroxiam's own words which made him take his hand away from his face. "What did you just say?" Laroxiam asked as he looked over at them. "That's what you told me; you'd do anything to get Emily back. If you succeed in this plan, you can bring her back to life." They explained which made Laroxiam think for a moment. Before he even realised what he was doing, Laroxiam already got behind the chair that the father was sat in before putting the knife over the front of his neck... just like he thought, he didn't take any notice of how close to death he was.

He looked at them as they just nodded back at him. Laroxiam took one deep breath and wiped his eyes as he had begun crying over the course of his thoughts... before he repeated those same words. "Anything for Emily." As he quickly forced the knife down upon the father's throat and slid it quickly across to the other side.

Epilogue: "The Beginning"

The bright and sunny weather quickly faded the second that he entered the fifth town with bloodstains on his clothes... or was it the sixth? He wasn't keeping track anymore. It all came down to muscle memory by that point; step after step, breath after breath, slice after slice. Within his grasp, he held two long, black swords that were relatively light with sharp edges pointing out of the sides of the blade that made them seem inefficient as weapons... although, he knew from experience that they were very capable of performing their one use in life relatively well. His white hoodie and black trousers were stained red with the blood of those who he had taken the lives of. Laroxiam looked around at all of the civilians who were passing by without a care in the world, he pitied the poor things for living such meaningless lives. "Why don't you all just go and accomplish some kind of great task? Nothing's stopping you from doing whatever the hell you want so why don't you just do it?" Laroxiam questioned the pathetic beings who would not listen.

With a sigh, Laroxiam knew what must be done, he looked over to his left to see them watching him from a distance before he slowly closed his eyes. "You don't enjoy this, you hate doing this but you know that the ends justify the means." Laroxiam told himself as the crackling began to start already. He opened his eyes and stared at the surrounding chaos that was happening simply because he was in the presence of all of these 'positive' things. All of the people were laying on the ground with the blood soaking into the earth and their clothes and many of the surrounding buildings were either engulfed with flames or completely destroyed. "I need it all, I need all of your life force so that I can make this world a better place." Laroxiam stated as he felt a rush of adrenaline throughout his body. This had happened so many times previously and his hand was moving uncontrollably thanks to all of the energy that was coursing through his veins.

"One more down, a few thousand left to go." Laroxiam stated as he began walking forward slowly through the town and onto the next one. "Laroxiam, watch out!" They yelled which caused Laroxiam to turn his attention to them. Before Laroxiam had even completely turned towards them, he felt a sharp pain that shot through his chest and spreaded outwards from there to the rest of his body. Everything suddenly felt like it was moving in slow motion as Laroxiam looked around at his surroundings only for everything to have an afterimage before it all slowly melded together into one single blurry mess. As Laroxiam looked downwards, the colours of his vision faded to black, white and grey before he saw a sharp blade-like object protruding outwards from his chest. "How... strange." Laroxiam thought to himself as he reached for the strange object before it quickly exited his body which caused him to fall to the ground.

"What the hell are you doing, Emily!?" They yelled as Laroxiam used all that was left of his energy to turn his body over and get a look at his attacker. Unfortunately, he couldn't see many colours so he only had the rest of their appearance to go off of; it was a girl about his age with long hair and she was wearing a jacket, shirt and some trousers... he didn't need to see the colours to know who he was looking at. "I'm sorry, Laroxiam... but it had to be done." Emily stated as she looked down upon the helpless, dying body of her former friend. Suddenly, all of Laroxiam's vision began to fade to black... pitch-black to be precise and as he took his last breath, the last thing that he could remember feeling was a burning hatred from deep within as they rushed over to him and looked him in the eyes. They said something but he could no longer hear them... but he swore that they said something along the lines of: "Time to return the favour."

Ever since that moment, Laroxiam has felt like he was in a constant state of moving between the boundaries of life and death; never dead but never quite alive again. He remembered everything that Emily had said to him as he tried to make some sense as to why she decided to do what she did. There was only one thing that kept popping into his mind; just before she disappeared, she was about to say something about the people of the world before she stopped herself and she seemed to have a moment of realisation. What did she realise right at that moment? She said something beginning with an F and an A. Laroxiam went through every single word in his mind that had those two letters in it before he finally stumbled across the one that made the most sense. "Fake." Laroxiam said to himself as he smiled and began to laugh.

"If you can do this because you believe that everybody is fake, then I can do the same thing for the same exact reason. The fakes must die, I will replace them with real people when I gain full control!" Laroxiam exclaimed into the darkness as he began to laugh uncontrollably. "Oh, my dear, Emily, you've made an enemy today. An enemy worse than death itself!" Laroxiam yelled as whatever was left of his sanity faded into the never-ending emptiness.